Senior Year

BUCKET LIST

J.M. MILLER

Cover photo by Regina Wamba—www.reginawamba.com
Cover design by Amy Queau—www.qcoverdesign.com
Editing by Lawrence Editing—www.lawrenceediting.com
Formatting: Champagne Book Design—champagnebookdesign.com

This one's long overdue.
For Bullet,
one of my very best friends.
She was the goodest girl ever.

Senior Year

BUCKET LIST

1
Celia

-now-

Life is a simple thing. Time goes by and you soon find your adult self in a usual groove, filled with ordinary habits and experiences, every single day. Routine. It's fundamental.

Wake up, work out, shower, dress, go to your all-around average job, take the next verbal lashing from your overpaid and under-laid supervisor, return to your spotless one-bedroom apartment, tend to the over-watered succulents, turn down the coworkers' spontaneous ladies' night and eat a piece of the lasagna you made and froze into individual servings last week instead as you binge a few episodes of that criminal show with the hot cop and sub-par plot, then finally settle into bed with every intention to read the self-help best-seller collecting dust on your nightstand only to download the latest rom-com on your TBR list.

Until one day you find yourself at your high school best friend's wake, standing at the food table beside someone dressed in a furry blue fox costume while "Highway to Hell" plays on in the background. Well … maybe that's all more specific to me.

Merilyn was an Internet personality. She'd always been adventurous, which was highly attractive to everyone within her gravitational range, whether they wanted to join in her fun or wanted to witness something extraordinary. It all started from day one. Being born inside of an elevator is front-page news in a moderately small town. I wasn't around that far back. I was a late addition to The Merilyn Samuels Show, entering in freshman year at Ellville High when my parents split and Mom moved us closer to my grandparents.

We all knew it was only a matter time before Merilyn discovered a way to turn her love of adventure into a moneymaker. At least she had died living a happy life. Or, I assumed she was happy judging by the content of her videos. It had been a while since we'd talked on the phone, and even longer since we'd hugged.

As soon as we graduated high school, we both broke free of Ellville. She jumped around for a year before hitting it big on Adventure Life—a division of YouTube for notable names in travel and extreme sports. I, on the other hand, stayed in Pennsylvania, driving a couple hours away to State College. And that was where I stayed.

When the blue mass of fluffy fur walked away with a full plate, an eau-de-toilette and corn chip scent trailing behind, I stared at Merilyn's senior picture propped at the end of the table between the quarter-cut club sandwiches and the Waldorf salad. Her head was tipped in the patent senior pose, long golden hair spilling over one shoulder of the photog's prop graduation gown. Her smile was natural, the same one I'd seen almost every day for four years, and her impossibly light brown eyes smiled right along, happy to be alive, happy to be looking forward to the next adventure—which, incidentally, was an hour later when her face collided with the assistant photographer's in a heavy, kiss-a-stranger make-out session. Don't be so shocked. Kissing a stranger was on our senior year bucket list. Besides, adventures didn't always mean physically challenging. Sometimes they were daring. And Merilyn was exactly that. Daring and bold, and as bright as a supernova. I had nicknamed her Nova for that reason. And though the name didn't stick, she wound up using it for her Adventure Life channel—Nova's Bucket List.

Here, right now, that brightness burned from inside a frame, even with a smear of Waldorf salad coating her cheek, looking a lot like something else if you get my drift. I giggled and slapped my hand over my mouth, feeling the immediate shame. But as I glanced around, seeing more tranquil smiles than frowns, I heard Merilyn's laugh in my mind and knew she would have stood right beside me, wiping the Waldorf smear from her face and laughing too. This was what she had wanted. A party, not a wake. People in bright colors moving in and out of the house while songs unfit to play at a funeral streamed from the living room speakers. Her parents had honored her final wishes, no matter how ridiculous.

I giggled again, unable to contain it. Despite what she wanted, it felt wrong to outright laugh at a wake. When I looked at the picture another time and felt the laughter bubble up, I dropped my plate and ran for the stairs, heading for Merilyn's old bedroom. As soon as the door closed at my back, I shut my eyes and let go, belting out a strangled mix of something between a laugh and a cry.

"This room's off-limits. Go laugh somewhere else," a somber male voice said. And though it sounded somewhat deeper than I remembered, I knew it to be Caleb's. He hadn't been downstairs at all, even during the eulogy.

My eyes popped wide to scan the room, noticing right off that it hadn't changed since Merilyn moved out nearly five years before. Caleb was seated upon the queen-sized bed with his hunched back to me, his black pants and dark gray shirt like a cloud of dread above the cheery purple duvet beneath him.

His head tipped back as he poured a drink down his throat. He slammed the empty low-ball glass onto the nightstand so hard I prepared for a shatter. Only, it wasn't the glass that broke. It was my heart, the intensity of his pain cracking me a little more when he spoke again. "I said, get out."

"I … uh …" My reply died in my throat as I watched his body turn to see who had intruded on his refuge. I looked him over as his glassy eyes zeroed in on me, noticing his disheveled appearance and the quick wipe of his hand over his wet cheek. He had grown since I'd last seen him. Taller and fuller. It was noticeable even without him standing. He was only a year younger than Merilyn, but that hadn't stopped him from being as popular in high school. He was the golden boy, and she, the golden girl. But now his golden hair had darkened, and his boxy face had the scruff of a man who hadn't shaved in days, possibly since he'd heard about his sister's death.

"Tar see ay," he whispered.

Of course he'd revert to using his rude-ass nickname for me. Tarsier. He had said I reminded him of the tiny primate because of my big eyes, small body, and because I was the quiet watcher among them. He always questioned my friendship with Merilyn and often acted as if I was a burden to deal with when we all hung out. Unlike them, I was not the adventurous type, and I would often mess up their plans in one way or another. But still, Merilyn wanted me with her and accepted me for me—not quite as energetic and usually the only one who was too chicken to take the risk. Much to Caleb's dismay and amusement.

I shook my head and actually thought of leaving without saying a word to him, but I knew that reaction would be a mistake I would regret for … well, possibly forever. Now that Merilyn was gone, there was a chance I'd never see him again. So I couldn't push my sympathy aside because of the small rift from what had happened—or not happened—between us years before. No, I wasn't heartless.

We both lost someone. He lost a sister. And I lost a friend, who had been the closest thing to a sister I'd ever had.

When my only response was to chew wearily on my lip as I made my decision, he thought better of his greeting and corrected, "Celia."

"Caleb," I replied. "I'm sorry."

"Yeah, I am too." He stood and rounded the bed. I stared openly at him, at the man he'd transformed into. "How long has it been?"

I shook my head and smoothed my hands down the front of my simple black cotton dress. "Three years maybe?" I'd seen him only a handful of times after Merilyn and I had left high school. "It was close to a year since I last saw Merilyn." I wrapped my arms around myself, ashamed at that fact. But she had always been so busy, and I knew better than to try and hold a supernova.

"It was months for me too. With her always traveling … But I suppose it was good to see her weekly videos. At least there was that."

I agreed with a solemn nod. "Look, I'm sorry if I disturbed you. I just—"

"Were laughing," he interjected. "You were laughing."

"Right." I smiled at Merilyn's dresser, at the picture of us at graduation, our smiles big enough to conquer all the shit life was about to drop on us. Feeling his eyes on me, I shifted to meet his gaze and was suddenly struck by how handsome he had become. Muscle definition was obvious enough beneath his button-down, so unlike the guys occupying space at Pearson Insurance with dad-bod, grandpa-bod, or workaholic-bod—except for Brent in accounting, who had the bod of a gym rat who bench-pressed big numbers at his desk and in bed, one number being me. I doubted Caleb even kept track of numbers. He was never the type to throw them around. And compared to my early memories of the gangly, big-eared eighth grader sliding through the same bedroom door with a squirt gun and a mouth full of braces, or the squeaky-voiced sophomore pranking us with shaving cream during many of our sleepovers … he was definitely a grown man.

"Are you going to tell me the joke?"

"No joke," I replied hastily. "I was observing everything downstairs. The music. The people. I pictured her standing beside me laughing and then started to myself. But I didn't want to be rude."

He rubbed the scruff along his jaw as the corners of his lips lifted the tiniest bit but fell almost as quickly. "It's gotten a little out of hand. My parents should have turned some of her super fans and video personality friends away."

"The fox."

"The fox," he echoed with another twitch of his lips. "I think that one might have been walking the neighborhood after an orgy and happened to find a source for free food."

I chuckled awkwardly then reconsidered my interruption. "Maybe I should—"

"No, please," he said, reaching out a hand only to pull it

back. "I didn't mean you. You might be one of the only people I've seen from school. She had so many friends. It's a little surprising."

"She did. You know most people got out of here as quickly as she did, though. They could have had issues getting time off or making the trip back."

"True. But I think it has more to do with the fame thing. She told me a good amount of people dropped contact. Jealousy. Anger. It bothered her some." He looked at the bed and nodded. "You want to sit?"

"Sure." I watched him sink down onto the mattress first before taking a seat and grabbing Mer's shaggy pink throw pillow for something to hold.

"It's unreal, right? Her life. Her death."

"Yes." My fingers worked through the pillow's strands nervously. Being so close to him had me worked up. It was as if it was senior year all over again. My thoughts instantly shifted to the bucket list, to one of the last tasks I hadn't completed until much later than senior year. Virginity. I'd nearly lost mine to an asshole who changed his mind at the last minute and never had the decency to tell me why. I could turn and ask him now, but to say this wasn't the time or place would be an understatement.

He let out a long breath, and I instinctively inhaled, smelling his cologne and the whiskey he'd been drinking, so unlike the cedar wood sawdust that hovered around him when we were younger. I shook my head, clearing away the thoughts that were starting to form. Merilyn was gone, and I was drooling over Caleb in her childhood bed instead of mourning the loss of her. Things were getting too hot.

I stood and moved toward the door. "I should probably go."

He was behind me in no time. "No, Celia. Just ... wait." His hand ran down my arm, drawing me back, asking me to turn around.

And so I did, staring right at his chest. I tipped my head back to see his face, and I was frozen there in his gaze, his light brown eyes nearly identical to Merilyn's trapping me for maybe the millionth time. There had always been an intensity within his, filled with determination, strength, and sometimes even desire. But at that moment, I saw only emptiness.

His arms wrapped around me, his head dipping low to bury his face into the side of my neck. He held me tight, gentle but fierce, releasing his grief and pain with long and steady breaths against my skin as his heart beat its brokenness with mine. I held him too, digging my fingers into his back, gripping him with a sorrow I had never felt before and with as much support as I could give as silent sobs shook me and tears fell steadily.

We were locked in time. I had no idea how long it lasted, but an abrupt shift in mood stole it away. Only it wasn't the break I'd anticipated, one that would have him realizing his mistake and disappearing, a reminder of that fateful night. Instead, his arms slid down mine and his hands trailed along my back. I shivered and cursed my body, unable to control its response to the closeness. With a sharp inhale, his whiskey scent filled my nose, making me very aware of every point of contact between us.

"Celia." My name was a whisper, as light as the fingertips skimming across the very start of my backside. His lips met my neck tentatively.

"Caleb," I breathed out and wobbled, hit suddenly with a need for more air. I was melting right there, under the weight of his toned arms and his smooth touch. I had never felt so damn good and so incredibly bad at the same time. Enjoying it was wrong. Enjoying it in Merilyn's room was even more so. I cringed.

He felt the movement and relaxed his hold but continued to drag his lips up my neck, scooping my long hair out of the way as he went. "Why were you so difficult? My crux."

Me? I was simple. A creature of habit. The one who showed up early. The one who kept promises. The one who was there that night.

"Tar see ay," he whispered again, his lips pressing below my ear before he pulled back to stare into my eyes. "Why are you so beautiful?"

I stood still as a board, my brain taking an asinine amount of time to process what was happening. My lips parted of their own accord, silently inviting him to kiss me while my brain scrambled to regain logic and reason.

He understood my invitation, and without hesitation his mouth was on mine, his tongue diving into my waiting, traitorous mouth. You'd think I'd have a little more respect for myself and for Merilyn—rest her adventurous soul. But no, there I was, gasping for breath as her brother squeezed my ass and worked my mouth in a way that made me want to drop to my knees and beg him for more. The heat threatened to make me combust on the spot. A tiny sigh vibrated in my throat. That only made things worse. His grip grew hungrier, his fingers digging in. I felt all of his length pressed against my stomach, and that only made me bite his lip to keep from whimpering with need.

"Caleb, I don't feel comfortable sitting alone with your—" A sweet, but irritated voice smashed through my sex-crazed thoughts like the Kool-Aid Man through a brick wall.

I jumped away, alarmed and embarrassed by my behavior, expecting to meet Mrs. Samuels' shocked stare. But it wasn't her.

Oh no, it most definitely wasn't her. The person was far from the charming mom I'd known all through high school. This was a crazy-eyed blonde in a black lacy dress, staring at me with the power of a thousand suns, all ready to burn me alive.

"What the fuck, Caleb?" she screamed then lunged for me, her hands reaching to grab hold of something. Anything.

I echoed her scream and ran the other way, darting across the room, knocking into Merilyn's dresser, causing a bunch of things to fall to the floor.

Miss Girlfriend, I deduced, was blocked as Caleb caught her one-armed and pulled her back to restrain her. "Jess, don't. Jess …" he said while she thrashed inside his containment like a rabid prisoner of Azkaban. He effectively herded her toward the door as she continued to hiss and growl.

"This is bullshit. I came here to support you, and you do this? At your sister's wake? You leave me alone downstairs and go make out with someone else?" she screamed out in the hallway with a huff.

My body shook while I watched the scene. I had no control over its response to confrontation or an excess amount of stress or anxiety. I never had.

This was not my life. Crazy. Unpredictable. I was not that girl, the kind who kissed someone involved. But he had made me that girl.

Dammit.

Staring down at the floor, I spotted a worn composition notebook with a cover ripped in several places and pages curling at the edges. Senior year bucket list was written sloppily on the front in Mer's scrawl with some doodles of my own making. It was fitting that everything would end like this. My best friend gone, her brother still an ass, and me … as sad as I ever was.

2
Caleb

-then-

elia's back. I stared at the pristine pair of baby blue Chucks lined neatly against the wall at the front door then kicked Mer's well-worn green pair out of the way and sprinted up the stairs, two at a time, unable to wait a moment longer to start the fun.

"Boom!" I plowed into Mer's room like I owned the joint. It was my favorite thing to do to get under her skin, though I hadn't done it much lately. Busy summer. Getting older. All that shit.

"Caleb! What the fuck!" Mer yelled from her closet doorway, covering her chest with a T-shirt that was obviously not on.

"Ah! Why aren't you dressed?" I yelled back, slapping my hands over my eyes and turning toward the other side of the room. "I need bleach!" I was so grateful there was no actual boob slip because of her quick reaction, but still … Ew.

"Why don't you knock, asshole! Mom's hearing about this," she snapped.

A giggle emerged from the floor, and I looked down toward

the familiar tone I hadn't heard for almost the entire summer. Celia lay on her stomach, her bare legs bent upward, feet kicking in a shallow scissor motion as she stared at the notebook on the carpet in front of her. Her short shorts had crept up, the hem cupping the crease at the very base of her ass, which was looking nicer than it ever had. She faced the desk against the wall, her head leaning onto her left hand, straight hair spilling down to the floor and puddling in a soft brunette pool. Fuck. I blinked and shook my head. I'd had thoughts about her before, sure. Maybe even a few welcomed dreams since she'd become friends with Merilyn. But this instant reaction had caught me off guard.

"You two …" Celia said, not even turning to acknowledge me. "I missed this."

"Yeah, I'm sure you missed Caleb being an ass and invading our privacy," Mer said, stalking past me, fully clothed—thank God—and shooting me an extra special side-glare as her fist slammed into my bicep. "You're such a shit. And you're dropping sawdust all over my floor. The least you could do is shake off like the dog you are before coming into the house. Dad doesn't even bring home that much crap from his shop and he's there all day, Mr. I Gotta Part-Time Job With My Daddy."

I rubbed the spot mockingly, letting out a not-so-fake "Ow." It did hurt a little. I'd rather sprint barefoot over a mile of Legos than admit that, though. When she settled onto the floor beside Celia, I moved across the room in front of them for a full view, then purposely shook out my T-shirt, watching the sawdust I'd smuggled in float to the floor. "At least I have a job."

"I'm putting in my application for The Shack this week. Speaking of …" She nudged Celia in the arm. "You should too. They're looking for carhops."

"That's a good idea," she replied. "I was planning to look

around for something when I got back. Babysitting gigs might be nonexistent since I had to bail on my regulars for the mandatory summer-long grandparent visit."

"It wasn't all that bad, though, was it?" Mer asked.

"Not really. Took some time getting them moved and settled. Their new place upstate is nice. Isolated. It's exactly what I told you on the phone. Boring despite what my mom tried so hard to sell me on."

"So basically right up your alley?" I joked. She was the opposite of Mer, completely happy with the everyday boring. Content with reading a book and playing with her camera rather than hunting for something to do in this small-ass town that both Mer and I often felt trapped inside.

She rolled her eyes at my comment, still not looking at me. "The time with all of them was good, though, since they won't be as close now. And I took some great landscape pictures to add to my portfolio."

"Well, I'm glad to have you back, Tarsier," I said, needing to stay in the convo and to rile her up with the nickname. "Mer was losing her mind without you, and that was driving me crazy, so …"

Mer let out a huff and picked up a pen to doodle in the same notebook as Celia. After a moment, Celia finally lifted her head from the hand it was resting on and looked up at me.

Holy shit.

I inhaled sharply, trying my best to play it off with a sputtered laugh/cough. How was it possible she'd gotten hotter in a couple of months? She'd certainly spent some time in the sun because those tiny freckles on her nose and cheeks had darkened up, demanding more attention. Her lips were parted, the lower plump one jutting out all pouty like. And those eyes. Those fucking bright-green rimmed hazel doe eyes of hers stared at me as if she knew exactly what I was thinking.

"Caleb," she replied, arching her brows in irritation. "So happy my return will make your life easier. Maybe you can reciprocate by ditching that oh-so-flattering nickname that wore out its laughs last year, one day after you so kindly bestowed it upon me."

"Not a chance," I said instantly with a smirk. Oh how I loved getting under her skin. Much more fun than irritating Mer or her other hanger friends. Celia's reactions? Those were like pb&j, sunshine, and woodworking—I lived for them. "Things wouldn't be the same."

"I can handle that kinda change," she retorted with a tilt of her head.

I coughed again and looked down at the book, needing an escape from those eyes. I loved every second they were on me, but today they were more intense than ever, making my thoughts wander, making things heat up all over. I pulled my shirt bottom out again, this time for a flash of cool air on my skin. "So what are you doing? School doesn't start for a week, nerds." Damn me to hell, I had to be closer. So I dropped to the ground and reached for the notebook.

"Nerds?" Mer replied with an audible pfft as she snatched the book back. "You're one to talk, Honor Boy."

Celia chuckled, the tone a sharpened lollipop—sweet but lethal.

"I know you're jealous of my intelligence, hater. But seriously, what's this?" They were up to something, and I wanted in.

"If you must know," Celia said, cutting those eyes to me, "your daredevil of a sibling has decreed that we create a senior year bucket list."

"Bucket list, huh? Like there's something or someone Mer hasn't already done?" I said, and they both glared at me.

"Now who's the hater?" Mer snapped.

"Okay, okay. I'll bite. What exactly is making this list?"

"Sure, there are some things I've done, but Celia hasn't—"

"You don't say," I interrupted with a chuckle.

Celia's face reddened. Her eyes dropped to the book, and she choked the pen as if she were imagining a grip around my neck instead. Crap. Maybe that was too far.

Mer huffed a breath. "Get the fuck out. Don't you have to get a shower and go hang with Sadie or Shirley or whoever your date is?"

"Shit," I whispered.

Mer laughed. "What a charmer."

"I would have remembered …" Had I not been sidetracked by the pair of baby blue Chucks downstairs. Celia bit her lips together and scratched another star onto the page. "It's Sophie," I added, feeling the need to explain for some reason. "And her dad ordered a dining set and hutch."

"So what? You telling me your part-time job at the shop includes turning tricks for pimp daddy Dad?" Mer laughed again then deepened her voice. "Tell you what, for an extra benji, I'll throw in a date with ma boy."

"Funny," I admitted, keeping my eyes on Celia's doodle progress. Star. Scribble fill. Tap. Tap. Tap. "No. She asked me, so I figured why not. If she has the guts to do that she might—"

"Put out?" Mer spat incredulously.

"No! Damn, Mer! She might be worth a chance. I think she's … nice. She's a sophomore. Not sure if she's my type yet." I pushed up from the floor and flipped onto my ass, kicking my feet out and leaning back onto my hands. "Just drop it."

15

After a few moments, Celia broke the silence. And even though I knew it was more likely meant to dismiss me than to save me, I stayed put, too curious about their plans to leave.

"So what are your ideas?" she asked Mer, tapping the pen to the page again.

Mer swiveled the book toward herself, wrote out Senior Year Bucket List quickly on the cover, then flipped it back open to the lined page. "We take notes on each task to keep track of progress. No need to do them in order. Variations of each task might be counted depending on the situation." She switched from marker to pen and started writing numbers down the left margin. "I can't think of any other rules right now."

"Sounds okay to me. I'll start," Celia said, her voice climbing a little with excitement. "Skip day."

"Tradition for senior year. That's a given," Mer replied, starting to write. "Crash a party."

"Ooh. Going big, are we?" I said with a whistle. "How about something more daring, like jumping off Eagle's Nest. We haven't done that one yet."

"True," she admitted, writing it down.

"I thought that limestone quarry closed because that one kid died?" Celia asked. "Also, it's a bit farther out of town. We'd have to ask someone for a ride if we have any issues borrowing our parents' cars. I know my mom will probably monitor the mileage I rack on hers. And I'm not sure how I feel about others joining in." The last part was a murmur. She wasn't exactly one to put on a show, so unlike Mer.

"That was a rumor from years ago. People still go." Mer shrugged. "And, I forgot to tell you the good news! Mom recently upgraded and handed over her ancient Corolla, so I'm in business. The boundaries for this list are not as tight."

"You mean we're in business." I checked her. Of course she would fail to mention the car deal included me. "They said we're both using it."

"For school and activities, maybe. But if I get a job, and if dad eventually gives you the old POS truck … Also, you aren't part of this. Go away."

"Dad may never surrender The Beast. And what do you mean I'm not part of it? Why?" I asked with my best sad-dog face. There was no way I wasn't.

Celia looked up, her lips curving at the same time. "You're not a senior." Her thin finger tapped the word at the top of the page for emphasis.

"True, but I refuse to miss out. I can already tell it's going to be amazing-ly dumb, especially if you all keep adding boring crap."

Celia's mouth popped open at my description, and Mer chucked her hairy pink pillow at me, which I caught with my hands … and my face.

"Oh, don't you worry," Mer said. "We'll do some epic shit without you."

"Won't happen," I replied, spitting out some pink hair before tucking the pillow behind my head and falling back onto the floor to sprawl. I knew Mer would fill in more adventurous tasks eventually, but I needed to be in on it all. Boundaries would be pushed, comfort zones crushed, and many first-times conquered, and I was all about that. Especially when it involved Celia, Ms. Inhibited herself. There was something thrilling about cracking the shell of a shy little egg. Maybe it was the process, seeing the raw emotion with each new crack. Or maybe it was the anticipation of the final reveal, what would be unleashed in the end.

"Get drunk," Celia added, making my mouth pop open this time. She wasn't the typical party type. Mer had dragged her to a few, but as far as I knew she stuck to drinks from the virgin variety or held a keg beer to fend off the offers until it was time to escort Mer home. So yeah, color me shocked. Those eyes were on me again and she arched a brow. She was happy with my reaction. Interesting. Maybe the egg was ready to break.

She tipped her head and added, "Get lost."

"Yeah, get lost, Caleb."

"I think that was for the list," I corrected Mer.

"That was for both," Celia replied to me, but turned her attention back to the book, some hair slipping the hold of her ear and falling in front of her cheek with a gentle caress.

Gentle caress? Wtf? I was losing it. Getting back on track, I said, "Ouch. But at least those ideas are a little better."

"Okay, smart-ass." Mer scribbled down more words. "How about climb the water tower? Get a tattoo."

"Hell yeah, now we're talking," I said, watching Celia's flinch.

"Good luck with that one, Caleb. I'm already legal. Celia only has a few months. But you have over a year." Mer laughed.

Celia chose not to comment on either the tattoo idea or Mer's verbal slap to my ego. But she did recover, choosing to add another task instead. "Kiss someone at the top of a Ferris wheel."

"Oh nice! I like that." Mer scribbled more words. "Kiss in the rain too. And maybe kiss a stranger."

I rolled my eyes and faked a yawn. "Enough with that girly shit."

Mer threw the pen at me. "Get out. This is ours, not yours. Go get ready for your nice sophomore."

Despite wanting to hang out longer, I knew she was right. About the date thing, not their list. I would definitely be involved in that. "Yeah, I better go." I hopped to my feet only to freeze. It took a moment before I realized I was waiting for Celia to look at me again, waiting for one more hit from those hypnotizing eyes. Shit. I was losing it. I'd always enjoyed when she was at our house, had fun messing with her—scaring her, teasing her. But it wasn't until that pause that I knew exactly how much.

Her absence for most of the summer hadn't bothered me. The return, though. It was like a kick in the teeth, heart, and dick all at the same time. Unreal.

3

Celia

-now-

"**G**irl, if you don't turn that damn phone off, I'll be forced to switch your margarita order to an Uber," Nadine said, waving her pointed and polished neon orange nails between my crouched face and the screen I had resting on the table edge.

"What? Are you too cool for us now?" Mina added, bringing my already unfocused eyes upward for the first time in several minutes, the bright red and white strip lights along the dropped ceiling behind her making me blink.

The bar area of our favorite TGI Friday's was packed. All bar booth tables full, and most of the bar stools too. Another Friday at Friday's. I giggled to myself.

"You barely spoke at work all week, your eyes have been on that thing since we got here, and you just sucked that drink down like you haven't had liquid all day. You're so focused on the screen, you've made Mr. Hot Bartender frown when he tried to snag your attention. I'm not waiting for the food to arrive for you to dish," Nadine urged.

Mina, Deandra, and Julie all nodded in agreement across the table from us.

They were my work crew. My ride-or-dies. Well, my ride-or-dies two nights a month at the most because all were over thirty-five, two married, three with kids. And I … I was the early-twenties introvert whose coworkers included her despite their age difference, interest differences, and all-around life differences. They were licensed insurance agents or underwriters who needed a ladies' night to get away from both office work and homework, involving something a little stiffer than the wine they cooked family meals with. I was the happy loner who needed to get out every now and then so she didn't feel like a total loser. It worked out. And it was why they'd been my closest friends since I started working at Pearson Insurance as a file clerk my freshmen year in college.

They all stared at me with the judgy eyes they normally reserved for my jerky division manager Jerry.

"What?" I asked, my head feeling lighter as I looked at them again, then tipped my glass back to drink whatever bit of water the ice had melted into inside the last sixty seconds. Where the hell was that second 'rita?

There were audible exhales of irritation—also usually reserved for Jerry, and maybe Fran, the big boss' bitch-ass secretary. Oh, wow, my tipsy thoughts had moved from melancholy to pissy real quick.

Nadine leaned her broad shoulder to mine, pinning a few of her long box braids between us as she tapped a pointed nail to my screen. She was the urger. The voice of reason at work. The one who spread her gentle toffee wings and tucked me under them, but who also knew exactly when to shove me from the tree. "Who's got you fucked up? We know it's not Booty Call

Brent." Someone giggled, and she shushed them with a quick breath. "As much as we'd like you to be done with that fuckboy … It's something else, isn't it?"

"I don't know what you see in him," Mina said, backtracking a bit to stay with the juicy Brent topic because she liked to spill the tea but kept her interest low-key enough to be tolerable. She ran her long, self-tanned, and ringless fingers through her straight black strands then tossed a glance toward the bar to see if anyone picked up her "I'm single" show.

"Oh, shut it. You know what she sees in him. We all know what she sees in him. He is damn fine. Did you see that fitted shirt he wore today? With the cuffed sleeves? Oh, ladies, that was too much office porn. I wouldn't mind being a notch in his bedpost either." Julie—Mrs. Dance Mom, drive-by PTO volunteer, and president of our office Jason Momoa fan club—said, popping her red-stained lips wide and fanning herself to ease that hot flush tingeing her alabaster cheeks. She was knower of all things man-sexy and a self-proclaimed expert in social media background investigation. Unlike Mina and Nadine, she wasn't single. All talk and fantasy, but she never crossed the cheating line.

"We do all know," Nadine said, side-eyeing them. "You all beg her to dish almost every time we're out. She's already told us she's fine with not being exclusive."

"You mean, she's fine with him not being exclusive," Deandra said then turned her large brown eyes to me. She was the calmest of them and looked the role too, with gentle features and short curly hair. Her demeanor matched her mama bear appearance—she always looked out for everyone. "You haven't mentioned anyone else. It's the one-sided part that makes us worried for you, hon. Especially when we see him flirting his way around the building."

"I'm fine. He's fine. It's fine," I mumbled.

"Yes, we know he's fine," Nadine said as Julie chuckled into her glass. Nadine arched her neat brows and shot Julie a look then continued, "But you most definitely are not. Something else is up. We've known you long enough. Tell it."

"I went to my best friend's wake on Sunday." I let the words spill like the tears had every night of the week, then quickly looked around the bar area, searching for that lying waiter who still hadn't brought my next drink.

"Oh God! I'm so sorry," they all said in a whispered chorus. Then Nadine added, "Merilyn?"

"She's the one," I confirmed. There were no other friends I spoke of to them. College acquaintances had vanished after I'd turned down enough party and drink offers. My routine was good for me.

"She's that Adventure Life chick, right?"

"Yeah." I tipped back my empty glass again, needing something to occupy my hands.

"Oh, that's so sad. She's seen and done so many incredible things, but she was so young," Julie said, already having pulled up Mer's channel on her phone. Deandra and Mina huddled closer to her in their booth. "How did it happen?"

"Ruptured brain aneurysm. Her parents said she'd mentioned having headaches but hadn't thought much about them. She didn't make it to the hospital."

Nadine's soft hand wrapped around mine. "Oh, honey. So this is why you called in on Monday and Tuesday. It's been a long week for you. I'm glad you still came out with us. It's good to talk about these things."

"Yeah, I probably shouldn't have used my last two sick days but ..." I looked over at the others as they watched one of Mer's videos. I'd been avoiding those since the wake, unable to convince myself to watch her yet. After a quick swipe of my phone, I was again staring down at my texts.

"That's not the only thing, though, is it?" Nadine whispered, noticing what really had my attention tonight. "Who's Caleb?"

The unfamiliar name made the others abandon the video and focus on me again, but I didn't care. There was nothing for me to hide. "Mer's brother. I hadn't seen him in a few years."

"And you saw him Sunday. Is it too painful to reconnect with him over her death?"

"No, it's not that. We, uh …" All of their eyes seemed to pop from their heads. Maybe that first drink was exaggerating things, but they were staring hard now, as if I meant … "Oh, God, no. We kissed. Nothing more." Although, there was no telling what might have happened if we hadn't been interrupted. "His girlfriend—or fiancée maybe—walked into the room during and freaked, understandably."

They all cringed with audible hisses.

"Yeah," I agreed, feeling the hit all over again. "He was drunk. We both were emotional. We hugged and then it happened. We have … a bit of history. But he didn't tell me he was involved. I'm still so angry."

"He texted. To apologize?" Nadine pushed on.

"He apologized, and he's asking to talk. He has something important to discuss." I rolled my eyes. Men. I swear.

"Oh, he wants something more, all right," Julie said with a suggestive laugh that was interrupted by the appetizer delivery.

"Would you ladies like anything else right now?" the waiter asked, setting the stack of tiny plates down then taking a step back.

I made a show of drinking my still very empty fucking drink.

"Oh!" he said, catching on to my desperation as he hitched a thumb over his shoulder. "Did he not bring it out yet? The bartender said he would. Hang on a second?"

"Yeah, of course," Mina said, answering for me with a flick of her hair before looking toward the bar.

"So what are you gonna do, love?" Deandra asked, her head tilting with the weight of sympathy.

Sympathy was something I didn't want. I needed to kick my butt out of the sad gutter, especially about Caleb. That was what the night out was for. I'd already planned on it. "I'm gonna give the bartender the meanest gaze imaginable when he brings my drink. Then I'm gonna down it. Maybe I'll stay for one more. But after that, I'm going home to my apartment to wait for Brent, who's scheduled to fuck me senseless tonight."

They all gasped except for Nadine, who narrowed her eyes.

"What? Tonight was exactly what I needed. Drinks with you ladies. Scheduled dicking from Brent. No drama. No strings. No hassle. My life. My routine."

"Well, that sounds amazing." Julie let out a sigh. "I might have to put the kids to bed early so I can get a good dicking too. If my husband isn't passed out on the couch already." They all started to giggle, and I felt the corners of my lips lift for the first time in almost a week.

As the girls started to talk across from us, Nadine leaned in close and whispered, "I can't help but to think you might need a little more than your normal plans."

"Nope, that's all I need. I'll miss her like crazy. Going so long without seeing her wasn't so bad knowing she'd visit again. Now, though, I can't help but regret the times I could have done more to see her. I don't know. Maybe that time away was a good thing. Maybe it softened the loss of her a little."

Nadine sat silent, letting my words linger for a few moments before she ripped me open. "I know you'll miss her. But I'm sure he's missing her too. And maybe, just maybe, that accidental kiss was only an accident, no matter what happened in your past. Maybe you should let him apologize the right way because, like you, he's grieving too. Don't let this be one more thing on both of your minds during your loss."

I heaved a breath, holding in tears so hard my eyes felt like they might implode.

"Ahem!" Mina cleared her throat and glanced around the table pointedly. "Well, hi there."

I looked over at what had caught her attention. Ah, the bartender. Holding my margarita.

"I'm so sorry this is late," he said, with a smug look on his face that suggested he wasn't sorry at all. Though, giving him the benefit of the doubt, he might have been before he caught all the googly eyes at the table. "You see, I wanted to bring this to you myself." He reached past Nadine to place the drink in front of me.

Sure, he was cute. Clean-shaven. Shaggy hair. Toned arms. Trim waist. He was getting Julie's eyes of approval, that was for sure. But he wasn't for me. Too unpredictable and lousy timing.

"When it rains ..." I murmured, noticing all the eyes had shifted to me. I grabbed the drink, lifting it toward Mr. Handsome Bartender with a sarcastic smile instead of the scowl he deserved for nearly killing my buzz. "This one's for Mer." Then I licked the salt rim, tipped it back, and downed half.

Though Mer was likely laughing and rolling her eyes at me at that moment while ogling the bartender with the other ladies. But no, not me. I needed my normal back and that was starting with tonight. No shifting off the paved routine. *Drink, home, a*

round or two with the fuckboy, relax the rest of the weekend, let the
Mer tears dry up, forget about the kiss with Caleb, forget about the way
he smelled, about the way he held me, about his sadness, my sadness—

Whack! The kick caught me off guard, making me spill my drink.

"Ouch!" I snapped, glaring across the table at the bitches I was close to hurting, only to realize they were all looking awkwardly between me and the bartender. "I'm sorry, what?"

The bartender coughed uneasily. "I knew I recognized you from the video. From the wake. You were friends with that Adventure Life girl, right? Merilyn Samuels?"

"Wake video?" I gaped. Wow. Things kept getting better and better.

4
Caleb

-now-

Staring up at the thin, iron-railed balconies and the red brick facade of the apartment building, my gut dropped. I breathed deeply and closed my eyes. "You have to do this. Dammit. You have to do this. She will understand. She will understand."

"She's not going to understand," a raspy voice cut through my murmurs, scaring the crap out of me.

I popped my eyes open and jumped back, dropping the goods in my hands—a bag of croissants, coffee holder with both coffees, and the single daisy. The splashes of coffee narrowly missed hitting an older lady who was bending over to grab a delivery box on the stoop.

"I'm sorry?" I asked, letting out a grunt as I stared at my ruined peace offering. Shit. Well, half-ruined. The croissants were in a bag. And the daisy … I picked it up and frowned when its head fell over in a sad arc.

"The girl," she said, tightening her paisley robe then crossing her arms while keeping the door propped open with her hip. "Cheap breakfast and a single flower." She tsked at me and shook her head of poofy brown hair like my grandmother used to. "That won't make her understand."

"You're right," I agreed blandly, bending over to pick up my mess. The lady likely had all kinds of boyfriend offenses running through her mind, pegging me for any number of them. I was guilty of most at some point in my life, but I doubted she knew anything specific. Despite the shit I'd put Celia through in high school, she'd never trashed me to others. Now, though? Well, maybe I wasn't sure.

I checked the croissants and tossed the coffee containers into the trash can beside the entry door. As I attempted to pass the woman, her arm shot out across the frame, blocking me like some apartment gatekeeper.

"Leann?" she asked, pursing her lips. "She definitely won't understand."

I pointed upward to the interior stairs in a silent question. "No, no. Celia is who I'm here to see. Apartment five?"

Her eyebrows shot up and her heavy-lidded eyes flitted toward the gray BMW I'd parked my Silverado beside. It wasn't new, but it was in nice condition. Celia's? I hadn't gotten to see what she'd driven to the wake. Regrettably, yet deservedly, I'd been getting my ass handed to me by Jess when Celia had left.

The woman's bemused look morphed into amused with a tiny smirk. "Okay then," she said simply, moving to the first door to the right with a neighborhood watch decal under the number one. Right before she closed herself inside, she let out a soft chuckle.

The greeting was annoying, but the thought of Celia having her for a neighbor was oddly comforting. I was willing to bet she either had a shotgun racked beside her door, a baseball bat, or at the very least a heat-seeking slipper. I shook off the nosy neighbor irritation and took the remaining stairs fast, not wanting to prolong things further. Extra time only gave me more of a chance to punk out. This was all so crazy. She had to hate me for … just about everything. And here I was, preparing to knock on her door after she ignored my texts and calls to deliver more bad news and apologize for … just about everything.

Stopping in front of apartment five, I reached around to my back pocket first, checking to make sure the notebook was still folded and stuffed halfway inside. Then I took in the no-frills appearance of her door. With a glance across the hall to another neighbor's, which was tagged with several peeled stickers and had a potted plant outside, I knew they were likely breaking the apartment regs. Celia would have decorated if she were allowed. Follow the rules, color in the lines—that was her, no matter how much we tried to unwind her.

Last, I did a brief check of myself. Non-work jeans and polo both clean. Boots sawdust free after their brush down this morning. Bag of croissants. And one sad motherfucking daisy.

"Dammit, Mer," I whispered, then lifted my fist and knuckled the door before I lost my nerve.

It was a moment before I heard a muffled voice inside. Switching the food and daisy from one hand to the other, I wiped my sweaty palms onto my jeans and stood up straighter, preparing for the disappointment, the hate, and maybe more than words to fly at me.

Instead, when the door opened wide, I was met with a dude's stare, not Celia's angered one.

He gave me a look-over, and I did the same. Solid build. Dark hair. Same height as me. Ordinarily, I would extend a hand, but there was no way in hell that was happening. His business shirt was untucked and half-buttoned, his jacket folded over an arm. I met his curious eyes before he took a second glance at my hand holding the croissant bag and the daisy.

When he only lifted an eyebrow instead of speaking, I finally snapped out of it. I thought it could have been the wrong apartment until I spotted a few recognizable black and white pictures hanging on the far wall behind him. Fuck. "Is Celia here?"

"Yeah," he replied with a stiff nod. "Hang here a sec." Leaving the door halfway open, he moved back inside and grabbed a set of keys from the edge of a coffee table. "C! I've gotta jet. And someone's at your door."

"I—what?" came her weak reply. After another few moments, she walked into view at his side, her eyes zeroing in on mine.

"Celia," I greeted her with a tight smile, not daring to use her nickname despite her wide eyes and the wild morning look I'd seen so many times throughout our high school years.

Her long tangle of sleep hair waved a little as she shook her head, closed her eyes, and bit down on her bottom lip. She didn't bother responding, but her eyes opened to him instead as he leaned a little closer and palmed her face.

He whispered something, and she replied, "No, I'm fine. It's fine."

"Okay," he said then he tilted her chin up and kissed her.

I blinked longer than necessary, knowing I should have looked away entirely. The memory of how her lips had felt on mine not even a week ago seemed to hold me hostage, though. A copious amount of whiskey may have been coursing through every part of me that day, blurring my very existence and creating a haze of chatter inside my head—spoken words of sympathy and mourning from others as well as thoughts of anger and agony from myself—but I remembered every fucking thing about her as if she were the rain within, clearing it all away.

Maybe I was as stupid as I'd ever been. She was involved with someone too. Of course she was. Clearly, sorrow had edged us both over a moral line, making us forget those who stood between us.

He broke away from her, and I couldn't help but notice the way her eyes narrowed a bit as if they held an unspoken question. Before I could think more on it, he was walking toward me to leave.

I stepped aside, expecting him to introduce himself, to solidify his claim to her with an introduction to top off the kiss they shared. Only, he kept walking, eyeing me up briefly as he passed. When I looked back inside, Celia had her arms crossed over her thin tank top, guarding herself and her bra-less breasts from me. I'd be lying if I said I hadn't noticed them and everything else as soon as she'd appeared. Her body was both familiar and not, and I couldn't keep my eyes from looking, wanting to remember all that I once knew, wanting to explore all that had changed … wanting what I'd never fully had.

"What do you want, Caleb?"

So much. "Can we talk? It won't take long," I admitted. If she was dead set on getting rid of me, I knew it to be true. As soon as she said the word, I'd be back in my truck, taking the two-hour drive home. I wasn't exactly sure how I'd feel about that, though. Torn? Lost?

"Give me a second," she said and disappeared behind the farthest door.

I moved into the living room, gravitating to the black and white canvas pictures. Looking over the silhouetted Ferris wheel first and then over at the second one with the face of a cliff and water below, I recalled exactly when she'd taken them. The sound of a car engine distracted me, pulling me toward the sliding glass door with its vertical blinds and pale green curtains spread wide. As I peered down at the parking lot, that BMW drove away. I chuckled. The neighbor had been ready for some fireworks.

"I guess it's my turn to ask you why you're laughing," Celia said, drawing my attention to the kitchen.

"It's nothing. Thinking about the pictures," I replied, steering clear of the boyfriend and neighbor topics.

She glanced at the pictures as she opened a Tylenol bottle. After popping a pill into her mouth, she grabbed a glass from the counter and washed it down with a quick swallow.

"Rough night?" I couldn't help but ask. In her minute away, she had pulled back her tousled hair, and also slipped into a bra. She looked tired and sad, and still as beautiful as ever.

"I had one too many." Her eyes cut down to the stuff in my hand.

"Oh, here." I set the bag and daisy onto the breakfast bar between us. "The coffees decided they wanted no part of this, so they offed themselves outside your building."

Her lip twitched the smallest amount, and her fingers bypassed the bag and lifted the sad daisy. Those eyes seemed distant as they studied the thin petals. "You drive all the way from Ellville?"

"Yeah, I live there again, inside the borough line. I guess I never really left."

"It's early. You didn't need to come all this way. I got your texts. Figured you'd understand."

"I understood." Loud and clear. She didn't want to talk, was content to never see me again. But … "But I did need to come. First, to apologize in person for what happened—"

She held up a hand. "Don't, all right? I never wanted to be an 'other girl,' if even for a single kiss. So whatever way you try to spin it, it's not going to help."

"I didn't come here to make excuses," I said in an irritated huff. "That's never been me. And can you honestly stand there as if you didn't kiss your boyfriend goodbye in front of me? Did you tell him about what happened?"

She smirked and twisted the stem between her thin fingers, spinning the droopy daisy head around and around. "Brent? No, I didn't tell him because he's not my boyfriend. He's a co-worker. And, not that it's really any of your business, we have an understanding."

Well, that derailed my thoughts. Whoa. I almost said it out loud. Celia having an open relationship or a friends-with-benes? You'd think I might be happy at that, but it only strengthened my irritation, especially toward Brent. I had some serious doubts that she came up with the idea. And who in their right mind would ever want to share her?

"So, you see … different." She dropped the daisy onto the counter.

"You're right. Definitely different," I admitted. "I know grief and whiskey aren't an excuse. I am truly sorry."

"I forgive you." She tapped her fingertips to the counter then finally lifted those fucking eyes of hers to meet mine again. Dammit. One look from her always had the power to jack me up inside. "Thanks for coming to clear things up."

Even though she was dismissing me and the logical thing to do was to leave her alone, let her go on with her splendid life and open relationship with Brent, I still couldn't leave. Mer had made sure of that.

"There's another reason I needed to come in person." I

lifted the notebook from my back pocket and dropped it over the breakfast bar onto the counter in front of her. As it slowly unfolded, exposing the cover, I watched her expression soften, the tenseness disappearing.

"She had a last request," I whispered when she didn't speak or move at all. "For both of us."

5

Celia

-now-

Senior year bucket list. The title was a time-travel beacon, calling me to slide even further back into the past.

"Mer had some requests in her will. One was that you and I do this again," Caleb said.

"Her will?" I reached out, pinched the split, curled edge, and peeled the notebook open, expecting to be hit with a new wave of sadness as the memories poured out. Instead, I felt a comfortable warmth as if I were being hugged by an old friend.

"Yeah." His voice seemed deeper with its softness. Or maybe emotion was the real cause. "There are some things she wanted you to have. I brought a couple. The rest is still at the house. I'll bring them to you whether or not you decide to do this."

I couldn't lift my eyes to him again. Not yet. It'd been hard enough to focus since he'd shown up, and it had taken every bit of strength I had in my hungover state to meet his eyes when I thought he was leaving. Thankfully, the headache I had was dulling most other feeling.

"What twenty-three-year-old has—" I whispered but

stopped. Of course she had a will. Most of her adventures had some level of danger. It made sense that she'd been prepared.

Caleb cleared his throat. "Yeah. It doesn't seem real, even now."

Closing my eyes tight, all the words from the list seemed to blaze into the backs of my eyelids. Finally, I opened them and looked right at him, no longer able to avoid that deeper connection by walking away or staring at the notebook. And, yep, his eyes were as somber as they had been at Merilyn's wake—and as easy to fall into as ever. But the sadness and exhaustion in them made me want to cry. The hair along his jaw and chin had noticeably thickened through the week, and his naturally golden skin looked pale. "What exactly did she want us to do?"

"She said that it was the best time of her life. She was happy with all the experiences she had in her career, but we weren't with her. She mentioned plans to spend more time ..." He cleared his throat again. "Anyway, in the event of her death, she wanted us to relive it with her."

"With her? Her ashes?"

"Yes."

"And your parents are okay with that?"

"They understand her wishes. She wasn't meant to be trapped in an urn."

"Yeah," I whispered, rubbing my fingers over the page, feeling the scratches and divots made from our pen tips.

"I didn't bring the letter. I can the next time, with the other stuff."

"What does she want us to do? All of it, all over again?" I tried not to think about the things I'd chickened out of, and the others that might be too upsetting to relive, especially knowing Caleb would be with me to experience it again. He hadn't been the cheerleader Mer had been. In fact, he had fun playing interference a majority of the time, getting in my head or under my skin. And that was painfully true with one thing I hadn't crossed off during senior year—The big V loss. "Some things can't be recreated."

Caleb leaned his forearms onto the breakfast bar and pinched his bottom lip between his teeth thoughtfully. "She mentioned visiting the places of the tasks we'd completed but was specific in wanting you to finish the tasks you weren't able to before."

"Why?" I whispered. "Why would she want that?"

"I've been trying to understand it myself." He tipped his face down and shook his head. "Maybe this is her way of saying goodbye. Maybe it's about reconnecting even though she's gone. She always encouraged you, and I … I didn't, and I'm sorry for that. For lots of things. So I understand why you might pass on this. If you decide to, though, we can plan the tasks efficiently, get it all done as quickly as possible so life can get back to normal for you." He glanced around, his eyes taking in my stuff, sizing up my place, gauging my life.

It was an odd feeling, watching him examine my space. I didn't care much what others thought of me anymore. My life was my life, and someone else's opinion of the way I chose to live didn't matter. But it wasn't quite the same with Caleb. He knew me, knew me. He understood a lot of things about me. He could push my buttons like no one else, yet he had the ability to calm me, mostly when the mess I faced was one he didn't create.

I realized then how difficult honoring Merilyn's wishes would be. It wasn't only about breaking my normal, content routine. There was a chance I'd be left hanging once again. That kind of pain was something I didn't want to relive.

"I agree getting it done efficiently would be for the best," I said. "Most of what we did is closer to Ellville. If I do this, I'll have to drive a lot."

"I'd be okay with picking you up or meeting halfway if it makes it easier."

"No, that would only waste time and add much more unnecessary travel for you. And, as much as I loved Mer and want to honor her memory too, I can't miss work for this. After an extended family trip, a sick winter season ..." And the two days I'd taken this week ... "I've already used my allotted time off." Jerky Jerry never bent, and I wasn't exactly indispensable. With Pearson Insurance regularly hiring students for my same position in different divisions, my job would be filled immediately.

"You wouldn't have to miss it. I know the skip day is on the list, but that was something we all did. We'd only have to visit where we went ..." his words trailed off, recalling the memories.

I nodded, considering it all. Was I honestly going to do this? How could I not? She was my best friend, better than any other I'd known.

"There's one more thing you should know. I'm—we're going to record it."

"What?" What? My voice echoed inside my head.

"I know it's a lot to think about. But her followers were close with her. Dedicated. Someone even put up a video from the wake."

"Heard about that. Didn't watch." I looked down at the notebook again.

"She partnered with a production company for her channel. They handled most of the work—filming, editing, location setups. I've met the two owners, Jay and Sam. They were able to get that video removed from the other channel, but her followers watched it before it was taken down because they needed to see something. Doing this will give them closure."

"I ... I don't know." The tasks would prove hard enough. Filming for others to watch? That only added more combustibles to the inevitable train wreck.

"Hey," Caleb said, snapping my attention back to him. "You can be behind the camera most of the time if it makes you more comfortable. And if you need a few days to think it over"—he pushed away from the breakfast bar—"that's okay too."

Shit. "Will anyone else be with us?"

"They might want to go to the locations for additional footage of the area after, but we'll film the majority ourselves and turn it over when we finish. I'm sure if we wanted to be more involved with editing, during and after, they'd be okay with it. That way nothing's posted without our approval."

I chewed my bottom lip and ran my finger over the page, tracing all the scattered check marks. Black checks, Merilyn—she'd done them all. Blue checks, me—I hadn't done nearly as many. And finally red checks, Caleb—he'd done several even though he technically wasn't a senior. I didn't bother turning to the other pages. They held dates and times, people and places. Notes. I wouldn't need them to remember, though. The memories were all fresh enough to evoke every emotion, every song, every smell ...

"I understand it's a lot to decide right now. I can leave," Caleb said, taking a step back and rubbing the back of his head as he looked around my place again. "You can call—"

"No," I stated firmly, closing the notebook's cover. It would be best to get it done as soon as possible. "I'll do it. For her, I'll do it. And I'm free today and tomorrow if you are. So where should we start?"

6

Celia

-then-

Breathe. *Just breathe.* There was no reason to panic. Not at all. I tried to clear my mind, ignore the creak the loose floorboards made with each tip-toe step of my Chucks, and of course forget the rumors about the widow who had hung herself years before. Supposedly, it had been inside one of the bedrooms upstairs, though. Not the living room, where I was currently hyperventilating as quietly and as shallowly as possible so the dust wouldn't send me into a sneezing fit and wake every ghost in the place. Walk in the park. No biggie. At least there were small bits of moonlight trickling in the creepy space by way of cracks between boarded windows, giving my eyes something to focus on.

"RAWR!"

"AHHH!" Ohmygod, ohmygod, ohmygod. My entire body spasmed then my legs seized up like a fainting goat, dropping me to the rickety floor in a frightened heap instead of doing their damn jobs and running my ass to safety. Fight or flight time and they decided I deserved the death of a horror flick chick. Bitches be trippin'. That was me. Officially a bitch.

Raucous laughter filled the hollow space, amplified by echoes. "Tarsier!" The nickname was barely distinguishable inside the fit of unrestrained laughter. "I really thought those big eyes of yours could see in the dark."

"Not funny, Caleb!" Stupid old abandoned house. Stupid bucket list. Stupid dare. *Breathe in. Breathe out.*

"You okay?" he asked through his dying amusement. I could hear how wide his smile was even over his creaking footsteps and the distant laughs from the so-called friends waiting outside the house.

I rolled my eyes to the darkness. "Dead to me," I muttered then yelled it out louder, "You're all dead to me!"

His breathy chuckle followed, and I listened closely as he continued his approach.

"Where are you?" he asked. "I had to hand over my phone too."

I held my breath, got into a crouch, and waited.

"Celia. I can help you out if you tell me where you are. Are you hurt?" His voice had quieted.

Creak. Another step closer.

"RAHH!" I sprang up from my position, my body slamming right into his.

"Ahhh! Fuck!" Caleb yelled as his arms wrapped around me, attempting to secure his balance. Instead, he managed to pull me off mine.

"Oh!" Unable to hold us both, I went horizontal for the second time inside of two minutes.

"Oomph! Ow," Caleb said, releasing a long groan after we crashed to the floor.

I started to giggle. "That's what you get. And thanks so much for taking me with you."

"At least I broke the fall," he uttered after a wheezy recovery breath.

A second later, his chest expanded fully beneath me, and I was suddenly aware that I was still lying on top of him.

He hadn't moved an inch. His hands still clutched my back, holding me securely to him.

Heat flashed through my body. No, no, no. This was not happening. Caleb? Mer's little brother? Master tormentor? I'd caught his eyes on me more and more lately—carpooling to school, over at their house, out with friends. And that was when he wasn't busy with an influx of interested girls, having gotten even more popular than ever after landing a spot on the varsity football team during the summer. It was hard not to notice the cheerleaders hovering around him—to include Marie and Elise, also seniors and our closest friends—all dropping by Mer's house more often than usual. And it was apparent that Caleb's ego had been inflated because of it too.

Not that I cared. He was Caleb, for crying out loud. The person I was into, who had no idea yet, was hanging with Mer and the others outside. Dean Paxon, fellow senior, basketball player, and who worked at The Shack with us. Mer had invited him and a few others to join in this bucket list task.

We'd already checked a couple things off the list, most involving school—attend a football game, take the SATs, college aps. The start of the school year had been busy with all of that, and with both of us landing jobs and her sharing her car with Caleb, it had been difficult to find the time to explore the rest of the list.

Until tonight.

Visit an abandoned place. *Check.* Unfortunately, that included getting the shit scared out of me and evidently falling on Caleb.

It was dark, but because we were so close, the dim moon-light peeking through the cracks in the boarded windows allowed me to see the contours of his face. His eyes were closed, and he seemed at ease, except for the fact his jaw was clenched enough to make his cheek muscles twitch. Having me on top of him couldn't have been too comfortable, especially after having hit the floor so hard.

Before I could get up, Caleb whispered, "See, Tarsier, not so scary in here. It's kinda nice, actually."

"Yeah, but … um." I shifted, meeting no resistance as his hands released my back, then got to my feet.

"Did you fall in a hole, Celia?" Mer shouted with a laugh from somewhere outside. "And Caleb, where are you hiding? I swear, if you snatched my phone …"

He stood beside me, close enough that our arms touched. His fingers moved, gently brushing mine then hooking the tips. "I want to ask you something," he whispered.

I was tempted to ask what, but I already knew. And once again I pulled a fainting goat, except this time there was no falling over. I simply froze with fear. Because for some reason I knew things were changing forever, which scared me more than anything.

"Would it be so bad, you and me?"

Thoughts of him in eighth grade invaded my mind, and I slowly shook my head in the darkness. "Caleb, I—"

"Okay, seriously. Where are you?" Mer called, and a light illuminated from somewhere down the decrepit hallway. "I already took my turn, so don't even try and jump out at me."

When I looked at Caleb again, I could see him clearly enough—his hat on backward, fitted tight against his forehead, eyes pinned on mine, head tilted, waiting for the answer to the question still hanging between us.

"I can't. I don't think we would … work."

His fingers slipped from mine then he took a step away and wiped a hand over his mouth with a nod. The light grew steadily at my back, brightening the room further, showing all the broken pieces of furniture that had been left behind, cobwebs and dust motes waving in the newly disturbed air.

"There you are. He scared you, didn't he?" Mer stomped closer, handed over my phone, then turned to Caleb. "I told you she would be scared enough. You can be a real ass. And where's my phone?"

"Yeah, I'm definitely an ass. Here," he said with a nod, then lifted his other hand with both her phone and his own.

He'd had them the whole time.

Mer tugged my arm. "We need to get going. If we break curfew and kill any free time to use for more list tasks, I'll be pissed. Elise and Marie left, but Dean is still out there. C'mon."

She pulled me, and I went along on auto, my brain taking a little longer to process what had happened with Caleb. He was left in our wake, but I didn't dare turn to see. My heart was heavy, hating the thought that I'd hurt him.

Sure enough, Dean was waiting for us beside his new-ish Mazda while his two friends Danny and Chris waited inside, their vape smoke spilling out of the windows and drifting into the woods bordering the back of the rundown house. His tall frame pushed away from the driver's door, standing full height among the reeds of overgrown grass and patches of wild daisies as we approached. He ran a hand through his dark chin-length hair, capturing escaped strands and tucking them behind an ear.

"We've gotta jet," Mer announced to Dean and she shoved me ahead.

My heart banged inside my chest. This was it.

I caught sight of Caleb in my peripheral vision as he stopped beside the Corolla, waiting to hop in.

"So," Dean started then cleared his throat. He took a few steps closer. "I guess I'll see you guys at work tomorrow, right?"

"Yeah," I agreed. "I'll be there, but Mer's off."

"Oh." His eyes flitted over my shoulder where Mer was. When he shifted a single step to the side, I knew, and my heart sank, taking all my breath with it. "Is it okay if I text you, Mer?"

The world seemed to fade away for a moment, my mind not wanting to face reality. He liked her. Of course.

When Mer choked out a surprised stutter, I spoke without looking back. "Yeah, it's okay for you to text her."

"Cool. I'll text you tomorrow then."

And with that, I wrenched open the Corolla's passenger door, vaguely registering movement outside as my body started to shake. I clamped my hands into fists to control myself. There was no way I'd fall apart over this. It had happened before and was one of those things that came with being Mer's friend. She attracted a lot of attention with her classic looks and carefree personality. Besides, it wasn't like I'd never dated anyone. I'd had a few dates. Though, it was my luck that it would happen again when I was going to make a first move for the first time.

The back door opened and Caleb hopped in while the Mazda started outside.

Mer opened her door and got in as Dean pulled away. She turned to me, but I only stared out the front windshield at the busted house, at its broken shutters and boarded windows.

"What the hell was that? I am not interested in—"

"Why not?" I asked, cutting her off. "He's a great guy. He's always nice to us at work."

"C, you like him. I would never—"

"I know you wouldn't. And that's why I told him yes for you. I don't mind. Honestly. But can we go, please? I don't want to be late."

After a long exhale, Mer glanced into her rearview at Caleb for a moment before starting the car. "All right."

The ride was filled with a soft hum of music and just enough awkward tension to keep us all quiet. When she pulled into an open spot in front of my apartment building, I jumped out so fast I almost fell over. But before I could escape, Caleb was out of the backseat, grabbing my arm. His grip was so gentle, I was surprised I'd felt it at all. He dropped his hold as soon as I turned to look at him. Without a word, he held up his other hand. Pinched between his fingers was a single daisy.

"I'm calling you tomorrow," Mer said through the open passenger door. "We'll talk more about this. Don't stress."

I nodded even though she couldn't see me then found Caleb's eyes and took hold of the flower he offered.

"Night," was all he said before slipping into the front seat and closing the door.

7
Caleb

-now-

The beat-up silver Civic Celia had been driving since she'd graduated high school was already parked on the roadside when I arrived at the vacant lot. After pulling behind her car, I took a deep breath and glanced at the contract from the production company. My thoughts spun. I was still so numb from it all and could hardly believe that Celia agreed to re-visit the list with me. It had taken me a couple of days to decide to do it myself and even a couple more before I had the guts to contact her.

Grabbing the GoPro, I thought about the production company's offer. They were close with Mer, filmed all over the world with her for the channel. So they knew the idea all started with the senior year bucket list, knew about her will and what she'd wanted us do. Which was why they'd contacted me, asking if I'd be willing to film it all for her followers. It wasn't in Mer's request, but she would have approved, as a way to give everyone closure. The money that came with it was simply a bonus, one I planned to use to help expand my father's company. Since Celia agreed to do the list as well, she'd get half. But after hearing her initial reluctance, it was best not to disclose all that information right away. She knew it was for Mer and her followers. That was the most important thing.

I looked at the silver and black speckled urn sitting at my side. Despite my numbness, feelings stirred inside. Love. Hate. Anger. Sadness. Mer had definitely made me feel it all. It was time to start releasing them and her.

Celia stood in the center of the empty lot, staring downward as I walked up behind her.

"There was Saturday traffic close to my place," I said, and she turned around. She'd showered and dressed after refusing my offer to drive. Her hair was wrapped in a messy bun with damp loops and end pieces escaping at every angle. A fitted gray V-neck and tight jeans accentuated all her curves, and a pair of flats had replaced her once favored baby blue Chucks. The smell of her soap or shampoo carried through the air between us, and I inhaled. It was as fresh and delicate as I remembered from the wake. I had to close my eyes for a moment to collect myself, to push the memory of holding her out of my head. Though, when I opened my eyes to the empty field, the memory of the first true time I'd held her close jumped right into its place instead.

She blinked at me, snapping my thoughts back into focus. "There was a ruckus close to where I live. Little dealers and their weekend lemonade stands."

Her lips parted and one corner twitched before she looked down at my full hands. "That's a pretty urn. At the wake, I thought about how well it suited her."

I held it out for her, and she tentatively wrapped her hands around the cool metal as if she were worried she'd drop it. "Mom picked it out. If Mer had, it probably would have had an inscription so she could have the final word." When she remained quiet, I added, "You sure you're okay with all of this?" The last thing I wanted to do was make her uncomfortable. Though, I guessed Mer wanted that for both of us. Otherwise, she wouldn't have requested we relive it all. Maybe some things were meant to stay in the past.

"Yes, I'm sure," she answered, then turned toward the overgrown grass. "When was the house torn down?"

"Two years ago, I think. It burned down, so the borough removed what was left. My mom told me about it, but I hadn't seen it either. I don't come over this way too often." I studied the GoPro, checking the settings.

"You said you have your own place?"

"I rent a one-bedroom cottage on a farm. It's closer to work. Dad upsized, moved out of the backyard shop. He leases a warehouse for both production and storage."

"I think I recall Mer saying that a while ago. I didn't talk long with your parents on Sunday, but I did wonder why the wood scent wasn't as strong inside," she said. "So you're working for him again?"

"Yeah. After two years at the Altoona campus, I decided to get back to work and finish courses online. Did you finish at University Park?" My attention had fallen away from the camera and had refocused on her, watching the way her hands cradled the urn, how her eyes roamed the overgrown grass then shifted to the wooded area. She was avoiding me like she had inside her apartment, looking at anything else. I couldn't blame her after what I'd done. Before she agreed to relive the list, she'd been prepared to never see me again. And damn, knowing that did hurt.

"Yeah. Bachelor of Design. Photography."

"Right. Pretty sure Mer mentioned. What's the gig then?"

"I, uh, work at an insurance company, actually. It's the job I had through school, and I just kinda stayed."

"Oh. Nice." And that was where Brent worked too. I grimaced to the ground, wanting to ask more, to find out the reason she hadn't left that job for something related to her degree. Was it him?

She cleared her throat and looked back at me. "So maybe we should get started if we wanna hit the school and somewhere else today."

"Right," I agreed, holding out the GoPro for her to take.

She handed me the urn first then grabbed hold of the camera. "How exactly is this working? Did they give you any direction at all?"

"To be as natural as possible. We can talk about Mer or the list as much or as little as we want as long as we at least explain the task. They can dub more audio later if needed and take care of the rest."

"Is the GoPro the only equipment they gave you?"

"They gave me some other things. A small light attachment. A tripod. I doubt we'll need any of it. And you'll have to sign the release contract in my truck. If you want to have a lawyer take a look at it first, that's no problem."

She shook her head. "If Mer trusted them, if you trust them, I'm okay with signing."

"Okay." I gripped the urn tighter and took a deep breath.

"All right. Where do you want to do this one, right here? I need to switch the angle away from the direct sunlight." She shifted around, suddenly struck with a purpose during this odd situation. The ease that washed over her was instant. All the stiffness left her muscles, loosening her rigid posture, dropping her tense shoulders. It was nice to see her behind a camera again. It was like we'd stepped back in time.

"Has it been a while?" I asked as she moved closer and then backed away, testing the position.

Her eyes lifted from the tiny screen on the back of the camera and narrowed. "Well, I am a little rusty, but I'm more than capable of handling this."

"I'm sorry. I didn't mean it that way. It's how you reacted. Maybe I misread …" Cue the awkward silence. Fuck. I shook my head.

"No, it's fine. But yeah, it has been a while."

"Well, it suits you like it always did. And if you'd be more comfortable using your camera, I'm sure they wouldn't care. As long as the footage is good."

After a couple blinks, she refocused on the task, and I heaved a sigh.

"All right. I think we can start. We don't need a wide angle for this, so I switched the settings. I'm ready when you are."

She lifted her hand to indicate she had started filming, and I jumped in.

"Hi. I'm Caleb Samuels. You all knew my sister, Merilyn, from watching her Adventure Life channel Nova's Bucket List, which you're probably watching this on." After a pause and a deep breath, I continued, "I wish I didn't have to be here right now, wish we didn't have to say goodbye. But …" I held up the urn and pinched my lips together. "She wanted to have one last adventure with me and our friend, Celia, to revisit something that helped kick-start her obsession with adventure and her love of sharing it all with you." I reached into my back pocket with my free hand and grabbed the notebook. "This is her senior year bucket list."

8

Celia

-now-

I felt so conflicted as I watched him speak to the camera. There was a part of me that had always loved him, as a friend and more. It was difficult to be so close and ignore the flutter in my stomach, the rush of heat through my body, the memories of his arms around me while he whispered into my ear and skimmed his lips along my neck. But I'd always hated him too. Hated the times he'd pushed me, taunted me, angered me, and most of all how he'd crushed me. And now, I hated him even more for making me feel like a piece of trash, another boyfriend thieving ho at his sister's wake.

He was a natural in front of the camera, like Mer had been, as if he'd done it for years, as if it were his audience and not hers. He held his sadness in well, focusing more on the task of explanation and less on emotional reflection. I could still see it, though, the pain and the struggle to hold it all together behind his eyes.

But no matter how handsome he was or how much I longed to express my empathy, I couldn't let myself be pulled into him again. Fool me once, fool me twice. It was high time I learned this damn lesson before I allowed my heart to be broken again.

Luckily, he'd offered me the chance to film most everything, except for the tasks I'd need to complete. Being behind the camera was not only better suited for me, but it allowed me to stay somewhat detached—from him, from the experience. I knew I lacked the strength he had and would likely crumble beneath the memories as soon as I tried to talk about them.

"So as you can see, the house is gone now. Because it's a task Celia and I completed with Mer, we won't be seeking out another abandoned place to visit. As she requested, we're going to leave a little bit of her behind." Caleb unscrewed the top of the urn and tipped it, allowing some of the ashes to fall.

Since there was no zoom on the GoPro, I tightened the shot by stepping closer, catching the beauty and the sadness of the moment as the tiny particles wafted down to the overgrown reedy grass.

After he screwed the top back into place and looked over the grounds, he turned back to me with a nod.

"That was good," I said, clearing the emotional lump in my throat with a little cough. "Should we head to the school next then?"

He nodded, and we both walked away from the area where the house once sat, where I'd once thought I made the worst decision of my life. I changed my mind later, of course, after I'd been scorned. But now I knew it all happened for a reason, not that I had any idea of what that reason was anymore.

Our plan for the list was to handle most of the completed tasks first. Visit the places. Scatter the ashes. I'd hoped reliving those memories and having that time to adjust would help me prepare for the things I still had to accomplish. Those tasks would be harder to complete, and the memories even more challenging to face.

"Before I forget to grab it again, here's the contract," Caleb said, exiting his truck in Ellville High's empty side lot and handing over a small stack of papers.

"Thanks." I skimmed and signed, not wanting to delay things further. After handing it back, I stared across the parking area at the massive brick building where I'd spent four decently normal years of my life. They'd restyled the main entry with river rock accents around the pillars. Aside from that, it all looked the same. The lone beech tree at the corner of the parking lot had grown, though. "I don't remember it being so tall." The canopy was wide, shading the immediate area fully from the warm springtime sun.

"Kinda crazy how much can change in five years, right?" he said, stepping off the pavement, closer to the tree.

"Kinda crazy how much doesn't," I added, looking around.

"True." His voice was almost a whisper, and I couldn't bring myself to turn around to him.

Instead, I lifted the camera and filmed a sweeping shot of the high school's main entrance. When I finally turned, his eyes were exactly where I thought they'd be. On me.

He blinked a few times then moved to the tree and spread a hand over the blue-gray bark. It should have been fairly smooth, but more carvings had been made.

"Whoa," I murmured. "There are a lot more names there."

"Yeah, the list sort of became a thing after you and Mer left. Many made their own. Some even tried to recreate ours, after either being with us for one of the tasks or hearing about it. I think the abandoned house was a casualty of that."

"Really? I had no idea. Guess I kinda detached from here

entirely after I left and my mom moved upstate to be closer to my grandparents again."

"I remember, yeah. How is everyone?"

"Good. Nothing noteworthy. I visit when I have time off."

"That's great. Tell your mom hi for me?"

"Sure," I agreed, stepping up to the tree. "I still find it weird that others jumped into the list idea. I suppose Mer's channel taking off a year later helped too."

"That played a part, but it had already started for the people who had been around us."

"Did you do anything for your senior year?" I asked as I moved around to the opposite side of the trunk and stared up into the thick foliage. I recalled the day we carved our names. It was late fall, and the leaves had already turned from dark green to bright, blazing shades of copper. In the early afternoon sunlight, after school had let out, we stood beneath the fiery leaves with little survival knives or screwdrivers from the toolbox of some-one's car and dug our names into the bark.

"I didn't, no. There wasn't much I wanted to do except play ball and work." His voice sounded flat and distant, but I didn't question it. I wondered, though, if he regretted what he'd done to me. Wondered if he'd thought about it as much as the spiteful part of me wanted him to.

I trailed my fingers along the bark, following the divots and ridges of names until I finally found Merilyn's beside Dean's. "Here she is."

He walked around behind me silently, looking where I pointed. I stepped to the left and shifted my hand down, finding my own name alone with a small heart etched at the side. And over another step, below a few others, was a heart with the names Caleb and Marie. A junior footballer and his senior cheerleader.

"Should we get to this?" he asked, pulling my thoughts from the past.

"Yeah. I'll move back a bit." I took a few steps then held up my hand and started filming again, watching him adjust his shirt before beginning.

"So one of the smaller things on the list was to carve—"

"Caleb Samuels, is that you?" a voice yelled from the parking lot, making both of us turn. A stout silver-haired woman had her truck pulled behind our vehicles, her head stretching outside the window to talk.

"Uh, yeah, it's me. Hi, Mrs. Katz."

"Well, hey there, darlin'. Who you have there with ya? Anyone I know?"

Caleb glanced sideways at me with big eyes then turned back to the woman with a smile. "This is Celia. She was Merilyn's friend in high school."

"Oh, dear, yes. Oh, and I see you have the urn there. I'm so sorry for your loss. I won't keep ya. Please tell your daddy that I'm still planning on buying that trellis so he best not sell it."

"I'll do that," Caleb replied sweetly with a full smile.

As the woman waved and drove away, a dark blue sedan also pulled into the empty parking lot, slowing to see what was going on before continuing on their way.

"Life in a small town, right? This'll turn into a weird rumor that my mom will hear about soon enough." Caleb shrugged with a breathy chuckle.

"Some things definitely haven't changed," I said as I held up the GoPro, remembering how well he and Mer were recognized. "And I'm not deleting any of that."

"Great. I'm sure Mer's fans will enjoy that small-town break from their usual content immensely, thanks. Actually, they might find it to be the best part of my exceptional commentary."

I scrunched my brows and my lips. "Caleb Samuels, did you just say something that lacked confidence? I'm shocked."

With a sly smile, he raised his brows dramatically. "Oh? Was I really that bad? Wait, no, don't answer that. I'd hate to open the floodgates."

I rolled my eyes before letting out a soft giggle.

His eyes remained locked with mine as the humor faded, the brief moment of levity dying quickly under the weight of grief, pain, and maybe longing for what could have been. And that last part was a floodgate that absolutely needed to stay closed. Chains. Deadbolts. That adhesive on product stickers that required a gallon of turpentine and a blowtorch to remove. Whatever it took.

I cleared my throat. "Okay, should we get back to this?"

"Right. Yes. They'll take care of it, whether to edit or to track her down to sign a release, so let's keep going." He adjusted his stance, ran a hand down his polo, and began speaking again when I waved a hand.

As much as I tried to remain focused, I couldn't help but study him, observing all the ways he'd changed. He'd relaxed a little with age, holding a calmer presence than his rowdy high-school self. While he talked with Mrs. Katz, there was a flash of the teenager I remembered, full of amusement and entertainment. And when he'd smiled fully at her, something in the back of my mind triggered, making me want to be on the receiving end. But this situation wasn't exactly calling for that, and for all I knew, there could be no interest at all. An apology was just an apology. He also hadn't mentioned whether he and the girl at the wake had split. One kiss might not have been a deal-breaker for her. Then again, I doubt anyone would allow their boyfriend to hang out with the girl he kissed the following week, even if it were to honor his dead sister's final request.

I closed my eyes tightly. There was no reason for me to even think that way. Why should I care? Why would I want to know?

For chrissake. I coughed and nearly choked on my spit. Why would I even try to lie to myself? He was attractive. Strong hands and tight arms with those sexy veins that caught the eye. Broad chest and shoulders, pleasant and not overly stacked from an obsessive amount of gym time. Yeah ... so damn attractive. But I would not go there. No, I wouldn't.

"You all right?" Caleb asked, staring at me.

Shit. "I'm fine. Yes, fine, sorry. The hangover is having another go." Liar, liar, not the cause of my pants nearly catching fire.

"You need anything? I can take you for some food or—"

"No, no. But I think after this, I should go home for the rest of the day. I'm sure I'll be better tomorrow to get more done."

"All right," he said with a nod. "I think I said all that was needed here. I'll finish with the ashes."

I nodded and continued filming him, feeling even worse for causing issues with Mer's final request. I needed to get my focus back on her and off Caleb. It would be a struggle, yet possible as long as we moved through the tasks quickly. And though it wasn't the full reason I needed to leave early, the hangover's leftover sluggishness wasn't helping. Tomorrow would be better. I hoped.

9
Caleb

-then-

The Ellville Lions didn't make the playoffs, but that didn't mean there wasn't a party to go to. With his parents out of town for the weekend, our QB Murphy threw the final post-gamer of the season, the absolute final for seniors who wouldn't go on to play college ball. Invite only, mostly the team and cheerleaders. I thought I was feeling it. At first, I was. It had only been a few days since I'd called it off with Marie, but Rosalina made her move right after the game. Her offer to take me to the party was hard to turn down, especially since Celia was staying the night with Mer when they finished work. I had to get away from the house for a while.

For about two hours I'd gotten her out of my head, trying my damnedest to enjoy my life without being near her. Rosalina was helping, with her long Brazilian legs, dress nearly as short as her cheer skirt, and a curly black mane that reached the top of her apple bottom. I still wasn't getting my hopes up. Marie had felt the same at first too, a good distraction, one I'd hoped would take over all my thoughts eventually. That hadn't been the case, though, and somehow I felt Rosalina would be the same. Another Caleb casualty.

"Caleb! Caleb! Caleb!"

Chanting.

What was I doing again? *Right*. The dare.

"All bets are off if you take a header on the deck, Samuels," Murph yelled up to me as he climbed out of his backyard pool. He'd made the jump himself a minute before—from the roof, over the corner of the deck, and into the water.

Shit, it was cold. Not wanting to sit around the rest of the night soaking wet, I'd stripped to my Calvin's. The goose bumps on my bare body felt more like speed bumps, and my dick and balls had pulled a turtle retreat, seeking shelter as far inside as they could go. The first snowfall of the year made the roof tiles outside of Murph's bedroom window slicker than a Slip 'N Slide. My buzz didn't help my footing either.

"If I die, you win it all!" I yelled, and the small crowd below lifted their Solo cups or their phones with a cheer. This was going on Snapchat and maybe YouTube. Not that I cared.

Rosalina beamed a smile up to me, biting her lip as one of her friends leaned close and spoke into her ear. She was another senior who didn't mind hookin' up with someone younger, I realized. Was that some new subconscious thing for me? Dating seniors? Was I trying to prove something, to myself? Or to Celia? Age didn't matter. A single year didn't matter. Had that been her reason? I really didn't know. She'd said we wouldn't work. Maybe it was more than that. Maybe it was the "my best friend's brother" thing. Either way, I wouldn't know unless I asked, and that shit wasn't happening. We hadn't spoken alone since that night.

And then, like the magic karma fairy had plucked the

thoughts right out of my head, Celia appeared in the backyard with Mer, walking close to the pool where Rosalina stood with her flirty smile still only for me. Fuck me. Celia had gotten changed after work, ditching The Shack's black pants and green and white striped T-shirt work uniform for a pair of shredded jeans and a wide-neck sweater that had a lace tie up on the upper half. Was it new? The top threading was loose, and I could almost see down inside from my angle with the back patio lights casting over her. Her hair was loose too, hanging down her back in the soft waves likely made from her work bun.

My dick twitched, suddenly deciding that maybe it wasn't so cold after all. Shit. I cupped myself, knowing I needed to jump before I was standing over most of the party being filmed with a hard-on.

"Go!" someone shouted as I backed up a few steps then pushed forward.

It was all going well until I hit the edge. One foot slipped as I leapt, tilting me off balance, sending me into a twist. I heard the gasps as I went with the spin. There had been no sense in fighting it. If I had, my momentum would have crapped out and Murph would have been peeling me off the deck after collecting those bills.

I didn't see the water until I hit it, spinning perfectly into position to smack the surface with a full frontal flop. Motherfucker. The stinging pain stretched across every inch of affected skin and even wrapped around to my backside, as if those nerves were acting out of commiseration, taking some of the hit so my front would be able to feel again within a month or so. Part of me wanted to suck in a breath, but then my foggy thoughts reminded me I was still beneath the surface. The muffled screams were also a reminder. They had gotten a show all right.

After a few more breathless moments of shame, I pushed up to face the music.

"Holy shit, white boy!" Murph hollered, smacking his bare stomach before he doubled over in a fit of laughter, his hot breath blowing smoke into the cold air.

I wiped my hand over my face, clearing away some water. "What's my score?"

"Ten, fucker. Ten!" His swim shorts were still dripping, though he didn't look cold. A good laugh and a few beers will take it all away.

So will a full slap to the body and the ego, apparently, because I was roasty toasty despite the unheated water. I swam to the edge, pulled myself up, then shook off like a dog to wet anyone within proximity.

Rosalina was on me in no time with a full beer in hand. "Caleb, are you okay? Your whole chest is red," she said, leaning in close and running her fingers over the ridges of my abs. I nearly hissed from the contact, my nerves not numb at all. After handing off the beer and letting me take down half, her hands traced up my body then hooked around my neck, bringing my face down for a kiss. Soft, warm lips worked mine smoothly, giving me a taste of whatever fruity drink she'd had. "Let's go inside and get you warmed up."

I glanced at the house, spotting Mer and Celia. Mer smiled and shook her head at my idiocy. Celia's large eyes cut away quickly, as if she were embarrassed to be caught staring.

"Yeah, let's go," I agreed, grabbing Rosalina's hand and leading the way. Mer and Celia were right in front of us, and I felt keyed up enough to start something.

"Real smooth," Mer said with a laugh and tipped her drink back.

Celia still wasn't looking. She scanned the party, drink clutched in hand.

"What are you doing here?" I asked both of them, struggling to peel my eyes from Celia as Rosalina tucked herself under my arm. "You weren't invited."

"Exactly the point," Mer said, nudging Celia with an elbow.

"We're crashing," Celia confirmed, with a hint of a giggle as her eyes continued to roam. "It's on the list."

Mer took another long gulp from her Solo cup. "Plus, we've already been here for an hour and no one's cared."

An hour? I hadn't seen them. Then again, I had been making out in the hallway upstairs for a while before getting dared to take the roof jump.

Murph sidled up with two beers, already changed into dry clothes. "Ladies," he greeted them. Having caught the convo, he added, "Feel free to crash my parties anytime."

"Thanks, Murph," Mer said with a wink. "Caleb's acting like we aren't in class with you and haven't partied here before. Pfft."

Celia smiled at Murph, and he stepped in and dipped his head down closer to hers. "You need another?"

Fuck me. Another?

Celia looked up at him, her eyes wide and inviting, though not entirely focused as her body swayed. She was buzzed all right. "Yes, please." She gulped down what was left in her cup then grabbed the extra drink he offered.

"Let me guess, another check off the list?" I asked, sliding the hand around Rosalina down to her ass. "Get drunk?"

"As a matter of fact …" Mer lifted her cup to Celia, who lifted hers in return. "Cheers!" They bashed them together a little too hard and started to laugh when beer sloshed out.

"Cheers!" a lot of other voices called out.

But my mind refused to focus on anyone else. Even with my hand full of ass. Dammit.

"List?" Murph asked, casually sliding an arm around Celia's shoulders. "I need to know what this is."

"Senior year bucket list," Celia replied, not brushing him off. Fuck. Fuck. Fuck.

"Oh, right. You two are doing that, huh? I heard someone mention the abandoned house the other day," Murph said, more to Celia than Mer. "What else is on the list besides crashing my party?"

"Caleb, you're shaking," Rosalina said, her voice barely registering.

And I was shaking. My arms, my legs—it all was on vibrate. But I wasn't exactly sure if it was from the cold.

"We've got plenty of stuff to do still," Mer added before taking a drink.

"Like jumping off Eagle's Nest," I chimed in, my eyes tracking Celia, waiting for her typical cringe over something dangerous. It didn't come.

"Oh shit! At the old limestone quarry? I want in on that. A little more challenging than my pool. Better not flop from that high, though." Murph reached out and clipped my still-sensitive chest with open knuckles.

"That'll be springtime so we don't freeze to death," Celia said, drawing all of my attention back to her. Had she not approved of our roof jumps in the thirty-degree temp?

"Yeah," I agreed, catching her eyes finally and having to pause to prevent myself from reacting. "Because we wouldn't want to chance freezing to death after we break our necks."

Annnd that got the cringe.

I smirked at her.

"Caleb?" Rosalina said, her hands snaking up my back and my stomach, leaning closer. "You really should get dressed."

"Yeah, man. Shit. You're looking a little blue," Murph added.

"Wasn't there something on the list about a pool, too?" I asked, not even listening to them.

That got Celia's and Mer's full attention.

Celia shook her head and crossed her arms. "No. Nope."

"Hell yeah!" Mer yelled, tossing her drink and tugging her shirt up.

I wrenched my neck back, prepared to turn my head, not willing to see … *Oh, thank God she's wearing a bra. It's basically a bikini. No big.*

"Mer! What the hell are you doing?" Celia said, her eyes wide, looking around as all the people started to notice my sister stripping.

Mer kicked off her boots and yanked down her pants faster than a dude about to get some. "Adding it to the list!"

"No, no," Celia said, shaking her head. "You can't just add on a whim. We agreed. It has to be in the book."

"Okay, you're right … but I'm doing it anyway!" Mer let a warrior scream rip and dashed toward the pool, her blond hair flying freely behind her.

"Yes!" Murph laughed and took off after her.

The rest of us followed at a walk, watching as Mer launched herself into the air and cannonballed the water, sending a giant splash outward, nailing several people who hadn't looked up from their phones.

I stopped at the edge of the pool's surrounding walkway beside Celia with Rosalina still attached to my body—though she was preoccupied, her head turned toward a cheer friend, laughing at Mer's performance. Mer broke through the surface, greeted by cheers. I watched Celia's lips pull into a smile, happy her friend was having fun. The sight stunned me for a moment. The smile was peaceful, honest, and so beautiful. And it wasn't for me.

"You sure it wasn't in the book? I thought I saw something about a pool. Jumping. Or being thrown."

I didn't give Celia's tipsy head time to process my words before I twisted away from Rosalina's grip, dipped in front of her, and hauled her over my shoulder.

"Caleb!" she shrieked, dropping her beer and bracing her hands on my lower back.

"Better toss your phone if you don't want it wet," I said, then lunged forward to sprint the final few feet to the pool, squeezing her thighs hard to my body.

More voices screamed around us, noticing what was about to happen.

I felt alive for that minute, holding her, running, ready to crack another piece of the shell, dig down deep under her skin. I didn't care about what followed. Repercussions be damned. I wanted to see her wet, get her pissed, shove her outside that comfortable box.

Maybe that made me an ass. And maybe she'd hate me for a day or more. We were barely speaking as it was, so what more could I hurt? I couldn't stop thinking about her, and she hardly acknowledged me because I'd changed everything and made it all awkward.

Hating me would be better. It was a stronger emotion, one filled with fire and passion. I would rather that than nothing at all.

As the cheers and screams filled the cold night air, I leapt off the edge of the pool and felt the frigid water rush up on us.

Beneath the surface, her knee collided with my shoulder and her hand clipped my chin in her swim for the surface. When my face hit the air, she was already at the pool's edge. Most of the party had gathered around, laughing and joking and pushing. Then came other splashes as people followed suit.

I waded my way over to the shallow end, watching as a wet Mer and dry Murph helped pull Celia out.

"Caleb, what the hell were you thinking?" Mer yelled while a few more people splashed into the pool behind me. Evidently, the cold water had taken her buzz away.

I hauled myself out and followed them. "I was thinking it was fun."

"Not fun," Mer spat over her shoulder, huddling close to Celia as they walked. "She has no other clothes, ass."

"She can have mine. They're in the house."

"Fuck your clothes, Caleb." Celia's voice was soft and shaky.

"I've got you, ladies. I'll grab your gear, then get some towels and something Celia can wear home," Murph said. The smile that had been on his face after we'd emerged had fallen right the fuck off as if he hadn't thought it was funny too.

Rosalina had rejoined a few of her cheer friends on the deck. As I passed to enter the house, she stopped me. "I'm not sure what's happening there, but I'm no hanger chick." Smart girl. When I nodded my understanding, she added, "We're leaving. I told you I'd take you home, so if you still need a ride …"

"Nah. Thanks, though."

I pulled a quick change and was out in time to see Murph leading Mer and Celia to the front door. Her hair was still wet, but she looked warm in a pair of gold and white sweats, the Ellville lion logo on both. None of them noticed me.

Murph came back inside when they were gone, finding me

in the kitchen with a new beer. "Yo, she was livid." He laughed lightly.

"Celia? Yeah, guess she has a right to be."

"No, your sister was the one who was pissed. Celia only looked … I don't know. Numb. Maybe she was just cold."

Somehow I doubted that.

10
Caleb

-now-

Murph's parents' house still looked the same. Standard country two-story in a spread out suburban development with HOA community landscaping and perfectly manicured front lawns. Cookie-cutter. There was nothing wrong with it, but they all looked the same. Felt the same.

As Celia's Civic coasted in along the curb behind my truck, I kept my eyes on the house and thought about the girls I'd dated. Like the houses, they were all pretty. Well-constructed. Well-maintained. And all the same. Like the furniture my dad and I made, too. Similar. Standard. None like the pieces I crafted myself, the unique designs I wanted our company to expand with. Different.

Maybe the houses felt different to each owner, but as I stared at them, I only saw their likeness. They were never truly my type. All of them. They had never been the one I wanted, the one I gave up so I wouldn't hold her back. At least, that was what Mer had told me would happen, and I'd foolishly believed her.

Finally turning to look at Celia, I knew now I wouldn't have held her back. She seemed as reserved as ever—staying near State College, holding the same job, same car. She was still comfortable, true to herself, and still more beautiful and unique than anything cookie-cutter.

"Sorry I'm late." She moved around the front end of her car, gathering her long hair and sliding it onto one shoulder. Jean shorts with a pink linen T-shirt was what she'd chosen to wear. The temperature seemed to rise in the time she'd exited her car, and I suddenly wished I'd worn shorts too.

"I had to charge my camera this morning. It's been a while since I've used it." Her eyes cut over to me as she shouldered the camera bag.

"No problem." I snapped out of my trance. "Are you feeling better?"

"Oh, yes, much. Thanks." Her focus shifted to the house set far back behind me. "We aren't asking to go into the backyard, right?"

I laughed. "Not a chance."

Her full giggle rocked through my entire body. Shit. It had been so long since I'd heard the sweet sound. The previous day she had let a little one slip at the high school, but this one wasn't as stifled as that had been. And it fucked me right up.

"Yeah, I don't think that would be a good idea."

"No, probably not." I twisted the urn inside my hands, finding comfort with the movement.

There were so many things I wanted to say to her, so many things besides the lame ass apology I'd rattled off the previous day. She wasn't happy with me, wanted this all over with as fast as possible, and I couldn't blame her for that. So I had to be cautious because somewhere inside I knew I couldn't let her go. Not this time. Now that I'd lost Mer, losing Celia again would be unbearable.

When the silence stretched a bit too long, I said, "I'm glad you're feeling better."

"Thank you."

"Are you ready to start then?"

"Yes. I'll keep using the GoPro, but I thought I'd use my camera for some stills if you don't mind. In case the production people are interested."

"I'm sure they'd like to have extras." I wanted to add "especially your pictures," but the words got caught up in my throat and I bailed out like a bitch.

She unpacked the GoPro and checked the settings. "Okay, I'm ready when you are." Her hand lifted.

"Hey. Today we're at a friend's house where two tasks from the list were checked off."

I continued on about the party, covering what was pertinent and trying my best to avoid anything that would hurt Celia's feelings. Though, merely being here likely drudged up the bad with the good.

The street was mostly dead until a blue car drove by. And then a few neighbors stalked us, using their dogs as an excuse to linger along the sidewalk on the opposite side of the street, stopping and staring.

"The neighborhood watch seem ready for a Sunday morning brawl. Mer planned this when she wrote her final request. She knew. Oh, she knew," I said to the camera, turning my head, waiting for the cops to show. "Okay, Celia. Are you ready to run because I think as soon as I dump some of these ashes we might be accosted by the guy in the windbreaker and his judgy poodle."

Celia's body started to shake as she held in her laugh. I bit my lips watching her mouth do the same behind the GoPro. She nodded.

And that was when a siren squawked somewhere in the distance.

"Oh, for fuck's sake. Shit. Okay, people, the party story is over. Time to go!" I twisted the lid and dumped some of Mer onto the edge of the front lawn, trying not to think of how jacked up it all was—leaving behind some of my sister to be blown away by a stoned lawn care specialist's leaf blower or be pissed on by an impeccably groomed fancy poodle with a bow tie collar and a monogrammed leash.

"Oh my God!" Celia yelled, sprinting around her car. "The Giant Center in Hershey is next, right? I'll meet you there."

I couldn't help but laugh at the situation, shaking my head before taking off down the road. Ridiculous.

Almost an hour later, I pulled into the stadium parking lot and killed my engine. It wasn't long before her car rolled up.

"That was interesting," I said as soon as she stepped out.

"You can say that again. Maybe visiting the backyard would have been better after all."

"Yeah, maybe. Did you see that rent-a-cop pass by when we left the development?"

"Yes! There's no way we can drive our vehicles there again. He probably grabbed our plate numbers and put out a neighborhood watch BOLO."

"No more parties for us. If they weren't inside, Murph's parents are going to come home to one helluva story."

She giggled and adjusted the strap of her camera bag. "They still live there then?"

"Think so. He left town a while back but visited last year sometime. Stopped into the shop to say what's up."

"Nice." Her smile drifted away, and her eyes did too, glazing over as if she were revisiting the past.

"I suppose we should get to it." I turned and stared at the arena. There were no events happening midday on a Sunday, but surprisingly the box office looked to be open, possibly for an event later in the evening. "This one's yours." When her eyes snapped up to mine, the glaze from the past had been cleared away by terror, so I added, "I wasn't here. It's not my story to tell. Your turn to do the honors."

"I … um."

"You can do it," I encouraged, stepping closer. "Personally, I don't like the idea of leaving her on the concrete. So maybe one of the tree areas beside the main entrance?"

"I agree. Much better than a sidewalk or an oil-stained parking spot."

I nodded then reached out for the camera bag and extended the urn.

After a visible deep breath, she traded out with me and stared at the urn for a few moments. "Okay. I think I'm ready."

We crossed the road that bordered the arena and stepped into the larger area of trees and small shrubs. Shady. Quiet. I refused to think about all the ways drunk concertgoers could have defiled the space.

"You okay there?" I asked, and when she nodded, I hit the button to record.

"Hi, I'm Celia Simmons. Mer and I were best friends and created this senior year bucket list together, wanting to make our final year of high school special. It was good that we did since we spent much less time together after graduation. Life, right?" She smiled sadly and closed her eyes for a few moments. "So we're at the Giant Center in Hershey because one of the tasks on the list was going to a concert. Caleb wasn't with us, so that's why I'm stepping in for this one. Not many bands were scheduled to play here during the winter, but we found out that Trans-Siberian Orchestra was and thought it would be a great way to kick off the holiday season. The night was ... chaos. Which you know meant Mer loved it. And I loved it too. Freaked out for most of it but loved it. Whatever could go wrong practically did."

As she laughed and started to relax, getting more into the story, I realized I was smiling. Seeing a little more of that wall between us crumble was indescribable.

"So basically," she continued, "we had to push her car out of the snowy ditch, where Mer ended up losing a shoe. We were late, wet, muddy, and cold, but we miraculously found the tickets. It was a great night. Another one I'll never forget."

I was so focused on her I didn't realize she'd gone silent again staring at the urn with a look of love. Not wanting to ruin the moment, I did nothing to disrupt her.

After a minute, she glanced up at me. The corner of her lips pulled up a bit. "Sorry. Got stuck there. I guess it's time to leave a little of her behind. I'm sure she's glad it's not snowing." She unscrewed the urn and tilted it over. Except the weight was misleading ...

All at once Mer's ashes fell out, a big heap creating a tiny white poof as it plopped to the ground.

"Oh shit!" Celia and I both said—her grasping at the urn, trying not to drop the entire thing as I rushed forward, GoPro gripped tightly and swinging with the rhythm of my stride.

A laugh burst from me as I dropped down to my knees with Celia.

"No, no, no," she murmured. "Oh, God. I'm sorry, I'm so sorry." Her eyes were huge and welling up.

I continued to laugh. I couldn't help it.

"Caleb! Please help me. I can't believe you're laughing. Please!" she begged, setting the urn down and scooping her hands over the grass to contain the ashes.

Although I had an urge to take hold of her face, connect our eyes and calm her, I followed her lead instead, setting the GoPro down and digging in, only able to think of how characteristically messed the situation was. "This is ... perfect."

Her face tipped up so close to mine as I continued to laugh and funnel ashes into the urn. Her stare was intense, focused on my complete lack of anger or sadness. And then she cracked. A giggle she couldn't stop broke free.

The shock stopped me for a moment, and I watched her dig back into the ashes, dragging her hands together as more giggles gradually turned into a full laugh.

"Perfect? This is horrible!" she said through the laughs, shaking her head emphatically, her loose hair falling in front of her face with the jerky movement, light brown ends skimming the grass below.

"No, it's far from horrible. It's ridiculously perfect for something Mer would be involved in. You know as well as I do that she'd be laughing with us if she were here. Hell, she'd be crazy enough to have tossed some into the air herself. So don't be upset, okay?"

As her laugh died, she nodded to the ground. "All right. I just feel so bad."

"No reason to. Look," I said, scooping what was left of the ash into my hand and picking bits of grass out before tipping the remainder into the urn. "We got most. See? There's a good amount there." I rubbed a hand over the grass to disperse what was no longer scoopable. "I know what we can do. Let's look at the list, for something you haven't done yet that you need to do. You can do it here and that'll even things out." I laughed again.

Her shoulders shook with her own little chuckle then she wiped her palms along the grass to clear them. "What is on there that I can possibly do here? I can't remember. Most I still have to complete are the big ones, like the cliff and the water tower."

I capped the urn then wiped my own hands clear before reaching into my back pocket and grabbing the notebook. "Let's take a look."

11
Celia

-now-

"Is that one really the only option?" I crossed my arms over my chest as Caleb looked over the list again.

I'd just made a complete ass of myself, dumping Mer all over the ground. It wasn't going well. If that blunder wasn't edited out of the video, I'd be even more mortified. Wasting time thinking about that wouldn't help right now, though. Right now, I had an opportunity to rectify my overabundant ash distribution by completing one of the tasks I had yet to do—like Mer wanted me to.

"I almost forgot," I murmured, more to myself than to him. "She did it the same week we'd made the list. It was the very first task she did. But I—"

"Refused, if I remember correctly," Caleb said, smirking devilishly.

"Not exactly. We knew most of the people we were around. But yeah, kissing some rando at work or on the street wasn't all that appealing." I bit down on my lower lip, recalling a few times in college when I'd been at a party and done precisely that. I was older, not quite sober, and … wasn't bringing any of that up to Caleb.

"Well, now you gotta. It's what she wanted. It's all right to hate her a little bit," he added. "I know I've been pissed at her lately."

"I could never hate her. It feels wrong to say anything bad about the dead."

"Just because someone died doesn't mean we have to turn off all negative emotion. I loved her, but I also hate some of the things she did, the choices she made, the choices she made for others, like this." He held the urn out. "I wasn't thrilled about it."

"Really?" My mind instantly churned up reasons he'd feel that way, namely having to be around me again.

"It wasn't that I didn't want to do these things. After what happened, I didn't feel the greatest having to ask you to do them with me."

"Right. I was a bit hesitant," I admitted, pushing my hair back over my shoulders. "But I couldn't say no to her last request. I owe her so much, and we didn't see each other enough … we both should have made more time."

"I know what you mean," he replied, tucking his free hand into the front pocket of his jeans.

With his face tipped down, chin nearly touching his chest, his eyes peered at me with a look I wasn't prepared for, one that seemed to collect all my emotion and offer up sanctuary. He wasn't flirting, but he'd never really had to, with me or anyone. A single glance or smile stirred everything up inside. And he'd always been so easy to connect with despite his relentless teasing. I'd ignored those feelings for so long during senior year, fought myself until everything snapped together in a surge nearing hysteria. So even though he was damn fine and difficult to resist, the bottom line was that I knew resistance was possible. Especially when I didn't have to spend too much time with him.

Ugh. With that reminder of our goal to get the tasks finished efficiently, I glanced around, knowing I'd have to kiss a stranger. The parking lot to the arena was relatively empty, but some people were moving to and from the box office.

"Okay. I'll do this—"

"Great."

"But you have to do it too," I continued. "Didn't she say we both had to?"

Caleb rolled his eyes. "I don't believe that was her exact request. She only said you needed to complete the things you hadn't done."

"Oh. Well, I think you need to do them too. For the sake of the video. I'm sure her followers would want us both to do them."

He gritted his teeth, his strong jaw working its muscles as he contemplated. "Fine. I'll do it." He shook his head, breathing out an amused laugh. "Let's get this over with."

I immediately felt better. At least I didn't have to be filmed doing it alone.

We started toward the box office. Feeling the urge to capture a few moments in still form, I pulled out my camera. The light was lovely, with the sun beginning its early afternoon arc in the sky. Short shadows good for composition. Intentional sun flare possibilities.

Caleb eyed a few people as they left the box office area, and I snapped a few shots of him, awed all over again by how photogenic he was.

"How are we doing this? You want to pick your own person?"

I dropped the camera from my face. "Of course. What? You think I'd let you pick someone for me?"

"No," he said with a laugh. "It's just ... shit, this would be a helluva lot easier if we were at a bar or something. Thanks for spilling a little too much Mer in broad daylight."

I gaped. "Low. That's so low. And I'm sure you'll have no trouble finding a woman out here as willing as one inside a bar." I'd bet on it. I also wasn't exactly thrilled to see it happen. Suddenly, I felt even sorrier for his girlfriend and cringed.

"You want me to go first then?"

"Yes, please do," I agreed with a smirk, watching an older couple finish up at the box office window.

I grabbed the GoPro from him and started filming.

He turned around, then spun back to me as soon as he noticed what was on the menu. His eyes got wide, and I couldn't help but giggle. He scowled then turned around again.

The balding man wore a short sleeve button-down tucked into a pair of tan khakis while his spiky-haired wife rocked a peach Adidas tracksuit. Both looked at Caleb suspiciously as he approached. I closed in from behind, not wanting to miss any of the exchange.

"Hi! I was wondering if I can ask something of you really quick. See, my sister recently passed away and left a request that my friend and I check off some things from a bucket list we made a few years ago."

They stared at him, waiting for the question.

Caleb cleared his throat and tried his best to not seem menacing with his taller stature. "Well, one of the tasks is to kiss a stranger."

"Come again?" the gentleman asked.

"Oh, you heard him well enough, Frank," the woman said,

glaring over at me. "And they're filming it. Is this the world we live in now? Degenerates." She yanked on her husband, pulling him down the walkway while casting looks back toward us to make sure we weren't going to mug them or something.

"That went well."

I giggled then pointed at the next potential victims of our degenerate behavior, this time two older ladies who were already eyeing Caleb from the box office. Their jeans, ripped and studded. Their T-shirts, vintage. I doubted they were picking up tickets for the same show as the previous couple.

"Hey there, sweetheart," the redhead drawled, sidling up to him as if she knew what he was about to ask.

"Uh …" Caleb was speechless for a moment, casting a glance back at me. Those scrunched brows and puckered, worrisome lips made me want to fall over laughing, but I held it together as he turned to face them again.

He started with the same spiel as before but didn't even make it to the end before the redhead swung an arm behind her to block her blond friend and grabbed hold of the back of Caleb's neck with the other, yanking him down to her red lips. His arms flailed a little as he let out a stunned, lip-muffled yelp, and that was what sent me over a giggle edge. I had to grip the GoPro with both hands to prevent it from shaking too badly.

He managed to break apart from her, prying her hand from his neck and retreating a step. "Well, that was uh … great. Thanks for that."

"Oh no, honey, thank you. It's been a while since I tasted something so sweet." She puckered her smeared lips and winked.

The blonde cleared her throat and smiled brightly. "You didn't happen to need two strangers, did you?"

A massive belly laugh escaped me, and the ladies joined in playfully while Caleb wiped a hand over his mouth and shook his head.

"Are you ladies okay with us using this footage on the Internet?" I asked, the GoPro still shaking with my body.

"Oh, yes, you go right ahead. And keep hold of this one," the redhead added, looking Caleb up and down before they both walked away, a bit more bounce in their steps as they passed a noisy bunch of guys wearing security T-shirts in the parking lot.

Caleb twisted around and snatched the GoPro from my hand when I started to laugh again.

"Laugh it up," he said.

"Oh, I am," I admitted, holding my stomach. "That was fantastic."

"All right, all right."

"Hang on. You still have a little …" I reached out and trailed a finger over the side of his mouth, wiping the smear of lipstick. He went utterly still, and I looked up to see why. His eyes stared right into mine as a shallow breath escaped his lips. *Oh.* "I think I got the rest." I stepped back with a quick nod, attempting to clear my hazy head.

After a few blinks, he said, "Your turn. Let's look—" His entire body went still again.

I followed his stare to see what had frozen him this time. *Oh!* The security guys stood near the box office window, joking with the person working inside.

"Fuck no," he said with a laugh and shook his head. "That's not right."

I smiled, rolled my eyes, and walked toward the group. "What? You'd rather I wait for a—what's the guy equivalent of a cougar?"

"An old perv," he said, following behind me, then murmured, "Dammit."

I didn't turn. I kept pushing my feet to move forward when they wanted to bail out. Truthfully, I still hated the idea of kissing a stranger, mostly the idea of having it on camera. That was terrifying. But it needed to be done, and I had to admit it was amusing to see Caleb squirm a little.

Moving up to the group of four, I was pleased that they looked to be in their twenties too, and not at all bad to look at. Their T-shirts were fitted and most appeared in shape. Not that it mattered. It was one kiss, not an invitation to date. My routine was already messed up enough by the list.

"Sorry, Mer," I whispered to the sky, feeling bad for thinking that way.

The four stopped talking the moment they noticed me. Faces and eyes tipped, glancing first to my flats then slowly making their way back up to my face.

"Hi, there," I said, watching all of their eyes shift behind me to Caleb, who I could only guess didn't look thrilled since all their smiles disappeared in an instant.

One in the group didn't shy away, though, taking a single step closer to me instead, smile back in place, now larger and stretching his smooth dark cheeks high under his brown eyes. "You need some help?"

"Actually, yes. This is gonna sound pretty odd, but I need one of you to kiss me."

After a stunned moment where they all looked at each other for confirmation that they'd heard me correctly, laughter ensued. Mr. Dark and Handsome narrowed his eyes. "This a joke?"

"No, it's not. See my friend and I have to complete a

bucket list. Kissing a stranger is on it. It needs to be recorded and will also be used on the Internet, so ..." I lifted my hands out to my sides and gave an exaggerated shrug.

"All right then, I volunteer before these assholes do," he replied, smirking back at them. "How do ya want me?"

"I ... okay then ... here ..." I stepped closer to him, planning my position and how to control the kiss.

"Celia." Caleb's voice was low with warning behind me.

I ignored his tone, hoping the guys weren't lunatics and wouldn't try something stupid in front of what was possibly their workplace.

"Your *friend* looks ready to slit my throat," the guy whispered as I pressed a hand to his cheek and the other on his chest to keep from falling against him when I lifted onto my tiptoes.

"It's fine. He's fine," I said, more to calm myself than him.

He had to tip his face down to me because I was still too short. His arms remained at his sides until our lips connected, then I felt his hand mimic mine, palming my cheek gently. He was warm and nice, and I was thankful there was nothing threatening happening.

But I'd almost thought too soon. Because as I moved to pull away, his arms cinched around me. My eyes popped wide, and I nearly panicked, until he dipped my body to the side and chuckled against my lips.

Sudden movements and voices surrounded us. Lots of "Whoa!"s were said as Mr. Dark and Handsome set me back upright and released his hold.

"Easy, brotha," he said to Caleb, holding up his hands and backing off. His friends, who had positioned themselves closer, did the same.

Caleb was at my side immediately, his arm sweeping me

backward as he stepped in front. His breaths were short and rushed, his body tense and primed. "The fuck?"

"Sorry," the guy replied with a small smile. "I figured if it's gonna be filmed, ya know? Better make it look good."

His friends laughed. I smiled at his bravado—even though it was a bit much—then placed my hand on Caleb's chest to back him up. "Hey, it's okay, Caleb. We're done."

"Yeah," he murmured.

I looked over my shoulder at the guy. "Thank you for helping."

"My pleasure." He winked then spun around and jogged to the entry doors to join the others.

After a moment, Caleb shook his head and walked with me to the parking lot. "Sorry."

"You don't have to be," I replied.

"I do. I thought … I'm not sure what I thought."

"You thought he was going to hurt me. Thank you."

When we stopped in front of my Civic, his eyes cut to me. "Yeah, I already wasn't thinking. Then he … I'm glad I didn't have to kill him."

I laughed. He didn't.

His eyes connected with mine and the seriousness there bored into me. And that was when I saw what had been drowned by sorrow since the wake, what I'd seen those years before. The passion. The desire. The intensity.

"All right, well …" I took hold of my camera bag, and his hand released its hold. "Should we meet up again next weekend? Saturday?"

He seemed to snap out of whatever was happening in his head and pulled the urn up close to his chest. "That'll work. The rest might take more time. I know opening night of the fair is the weekend after next, but we could get some of the others done before then. Can I text you during the week?"

"Yes, sure. After work is best."

"Okay, good."

I nodded and dug my keys from my bag. "I'll talk to you soon then."

"Yeah. Soon." He reached into his pocket and removed his own keys.

When I drove out of the parking lot, his Silverado stayed.

12
Celia

-then-

"**R**AWR!"

"AHHH!" My bladder nearly exploded from fright. I jumped backward, tossing the tray I was holding into the air, watching in slow motion as the order of two milkshakes and two burgers launched like rockets prepared to breach the stratosphere. But the tasty interstellar mission was doomed from the start, and what goes up …

I slammed down hard onto my ass, and the milkshakes came after, lids cracking open and spilling vanilla and strawberry all over my work gear.

All occupied tables outside The Shack burst into laughter, having witnessed the epic scare.

Caleb's laugh was the closest, the cause of my humiliation standing right beside me. "Tarsier, shit. You okay? I didn't think that one would have gotten you."

I lifted my arms, taking in the damage as the milkshakes soaked into my clothes, cold and wet, exactly like the late January night. "Yeah, well, guess it did."

"Here, I'll—"

"Celia," Murphy came running up, extending his hand for me to take. "You all right?"

"Yeah, thanks. Glad it's the end of the night."

"You have a change of clothes?" he asked, helping me pick up the remnants of the order.

"Surprisingly, yes. I'm going out after and didn't want to go home to grab my stuff."

"Where to? If you don't mind me asking."

I looked around and caught Mer's eye as she walked out the door with a replacement order for the one I'd dumped. She rolled her eyes then slugged Caleb on her way to the table. "I, well, Mer and I have somewhere to go then I'm staying at her place." I wasn't sure if telling him was the best idea. Technically, we weren't supposed to go ourselves. The water tower was on borough land and was guarded by enough No Trespassing signs even animals could get the point.

"Ah. None of my business. Gotcha. Maybe we can hang a different time?"

"Nope, it's cool," Mer said, walking back to us. "You can come with. We're checking off another bucket list item tonight. Water tower."

I scowled at her, and she stuck her tongue out. It wasn't as if I didn't like Murphy. He'd gone to the movies with us the previous weekend, and I even considered seeing more of him. But not tonight. I didn't want anyone witnessing the horror that would commence when we arrived at the water tower. Climbing it was going to be a major problem for me. I was okay with heights for the most part, as long as there was no chance of losing my grip on a wet ladder rung, slipping, and falling to my death.

"Sounds fun! Mind if some others tag along?" he asked.

"How many are we talking here?" Mer eyed the table filled with our fellow seniors he'd been sitting with.

Caleb still stood right next to us, arms crossed, listening to the entire convo. He usually didn't hang out or eat at The Shack, but he'd been with them too. Also with Lindsey, his latest date.

Murphy looked over his shoulder. "The people riding with me. Maybe two, three max. The rest have their own rides."

"I'm in," Caleb said.

Mer glared at him. "Not invited."

"The fuck I'm not. I've got The Beast tonight. It's another ride, which is good to have in case someone needs to take a trip to the hospital."

I cringed. Damn him. I looked over and caught his sly smirk.

～

The entire area around the water tower was deserted as expected. First, it wasn't exactly in the middle of town. There was roughly a mile of field and woods surrounding it. It was an emergency tower, used if water was needed for any outage or major system issue. And second, even though it was Saturday night, it was also the dead of winter, and according to most forecasts an ugly nor'easter was fast approaching. No one was stupid enough to be out. Except us.

I took a few more steps away, tipped my camera back, and snapped a few shots up to the sky, where the clouded moonlight shone onto Mer and the others as they laughed about their conquest. They'd climbed the water tower with ease. No hesitation. No fear. I, on the other hand, chickened out. Mer had sat with me for a while until I forced her to leave me behind. There was no way I'd hold her back. I'd sit and wait for however long, as long as she had fun.

After returning my camera to its bag, I slid my gloved hands into my pockets and burrowed deeper into my puffy winter coat.

"Brr!"

"Oh shit!" I yelled with a jump spin, realizing instantly that Caleb had managed to sneak up behind me while I'd been focused on the merry voices high above.

"That's the second scare tonight, Tarsier. I might set a record," he said, voice muffled. With a beanie on, a hood pulled over his head, and his shoulders lifted high to keep his mouth behind the zipper of his coat, only his eyes and the top of his nose were visible.

"Ha," I replied blandly, straightening my own beanie hat and tucking my hair back into my coat. "I thought you changed your mind about coming."

"Nah." He shuffled his boots in the snow a bit and looked up at the tower when we heard Mer yell excitedly. "Just late. Had to take Lindsey home."

I didn't reply to that. Her prissy attitude the few times I'd spoken to her made me not like her much, but she had some sense to skip the cold, wet mess of this night.

"So, not going for it, huh?" His words were soft, calm, so unlike his normal amped-up nature.

"Yeah, no."

"Did you even try?"

I huffed. "Yes, I tried."

"How far ya get?"

"Does it matter?"

His shoulders relaxed, and his face emerged from behind

the barrier of his coat. He inhaled the cold air deeply. "It does actually."

"Fine. I made it a few rungs below where the cage starts."

"Hmm."

"Hmm?"

"That's like twenty feet. It's … farther than I thought."

"Ass," I said, chuckling as I backhanded his arm. "It was slippery. And I couldn't rush."

"Understandable."

"Are you going up?" I asked as my phone chimed with a message. Pulling it out of my pocket, I saw a dark pic from Mer at the top.

Mer: It's unbelievable up here. You okay down there?

Me: I'm fine. Caleb's here.

"I was going to," Caleb replied as I typed. "Not really feeling it now."

"No? That's a shock. You're not one to turn away this kind of thing. Something wrong?" My phone chimed, but I ignored it.

"No," he said with a head shake as he glanced back up at the tower. "Just cold."

"Same here."

His body shifted, turning to face me fully. "You want me to take you home?"

"I … well, I'm actually staying at your house tonight, so …"

"Even better," he said. "Fewer miles, lower death probability." When I scowled, he smiled a little. "Seriously, though, I don't feel like staying. You want to go?"

I wasn't sure it was the best idea, but standing outside in the cold, waiting for Mer to finish having fun wasn't exactly fun itself. And I hated to think she might cut her time short because of me.

"No problem," he said, taking my silence as a no. "At least go sit in Mer's car to wait."

As he turned away, I said, "Caleb, wait. I'd like a ride, thanks."

I swiped my phone screen open to see Mer's text.

Mer: Is he coming up? Or pelting you with snowballs?

Me: He's leaving. I'm riding with him to your place. You stay. Have fun.

Mer: You sure? :(

Me: Yeah. C ya la8r :)

After grabbing my bag from her car, I climbed into The Beast—the old Chevy truck Caleb's dad had passed on to him—and was met with a dull mixed scent of flowers and cedar sawdust, though only sawdust could be seen on the floor and in the cracks of the single leather seat, no flowers or air fresheners. I almost made a remark about it but checked myself as soon as I realized it might have been residual perfume from Lindsey.

I remained quiet, unsure of what to talk about. And he mostly did too, content with the sound of the heated rush of air from the vents and a steady stream of music from the speakers. Everything between us had been weird since the abandoned house and Murph's party too. I'd been so pissed that night. Too pissed actually. Tossing me into the pool was a prank meant in fun, and I overreacted by going heavy with the silent treatment. Around others, he continued his pranks to mess with me, like the night's spectacular milkshake scare at work. But there had been a few quiet moments since then with the two of us alone, where things were the most awkward. The ride was a bit of a longer version, though.

Mr. and Mrs. Samuels were already upstairs in their bedroom when we entered the house.

"Is it okay if I get a drink?" I whispered to Caleb, setting my stuff down as he started climbing the steps.

"Like you have to ask," he replied, then pointed up the steps. "If you need something else before Mer gets home, let me know."

I nodded and watched him take the stairs in a jog. A vase of mixed flowers stood in the center of the kitchen island. Daisies. Marigolds. Small purple lilies. I inhaled a breath of them, knowing immediately that they had been in Caleb's truck. He'd gotten them for his mom. Despite his constant choice to irritate me, I wasn't surprised by his sweetness. He had picked me a daisy once after all, the night both of us had been crushed a little.

Not wanting to linger too long downstairs alone, I made my way up to Mer's room and unloaded my things. Even though I'd mopped myself up with wet paper towels at work, the stickiness from the milkshake incident remained on my skin. Sleeping comfortably wouldn't be possible. I had to shower.

Silently, I walked into the hallway, looking down at the other end of the house where everything was dark, hoping not to wake anyone. Light streamed out from the slight crack in the bathroom door. I gave a soft, swift knock first and waited a moment before pushing in.

As soon as I saw Caleb—almost fully naked—I dropped my pajamas. My legs failed to move, and my mouth failed to speak—fainting goat without the fall.

His hair was wet, thin pieces folded over his forehead still dripping. His chest was bare and slick, as slick as I remembered it being at Murph's party when he was practically naked in only his boxer briefs. He'd been wet, cold, and shaking when he'd slung me over his strong shoulder and ran for the pool. Tonight, a towel was wrapped around his waist. Low. Like super low. Like "my eyes followed the thin trail of hair leading down to the top of a patch peeking out above the fold in the towel" low.

"I—" I started speaking but lost all thoughts. It was as if I was back looking at him that night, only this time I was fully sober. I also didn't have Murph at my side to distract me.

Caleb's eyebrows were raised in question as he leaned a hip to the counter at his side. "What's up? You need something?" He licked his bottom lip.

"I knocked. I'm sorry."

"I didn't hear you," he replied with a small smile. "You okay, Tarsier?"

"Fine. Fine. I'm fine. But sticky. Still sticky. From the milkshakes. I thought I should get a shower before bed. I didn't realize you were in here."

That smile grew into a full, cocky grin. He knew exactly what I was thinking while staring at him. Dammit. But turning off my reaction was impossible. His body was tight and toned and sexy as hell, and he was also completely aware of that fact.

He wiped his hand over his mouth then dropped it down to his stomach, knowing my eyes would follow. Those ridges of his abs. That cut indent at each of his hips.

Nope. Nope. Nope. I chastised myself then snapped my eyes back up to his, seeing them flare. "I'll just wait—"

"No," he said, stepping closer. "I'm done. I left my clothes in my room anyway."

"All right."

It wasn't until he bent down at my feet that I realized my clothes were still on the floor. He grabbed hold and stood slowly in front of me, backing me against the wall. Close. Really close. I could feel the heat of his shower from his skin, feel the warmth of his breath too.

He inhaled, shutting his eyes for a long blink and dipping his face down closer to mine. "I'm sorry I scared you earlier. But I'm not sorry about those milkshakes. I can smell them on your skin, and it smells … so tasty." The last words were a soft whisper that sent a excited shiver through me.

I closed my eyes, barely able to process normal thoughts let alone how my body was responding to him. "Caleb."

"Yeah, Celia?"

My brain finally kicked into action, sputtering with frenzied, quick thoughts. What was happening? He was with Lindsey. This was all wrong. And I'd already told myself dating him would not be a good idea. I'd told him that too.

I shook my head. "This can't happen. We can't happen."

"No? Why's that?" he whispered. His body hadn't moved, hadn't backed off an inch. Even without him touching me, I could feel him everywhere, all over me, and it felt so good. Too good.

"You have a girlfriend. And I already told you I don't think we'd work." My voice was surprisingly strong since I'd become so damn weak for him.

"She's not my girlfriend. We went out a couple times. Nothing set or serious. And I don't believe you about us. I'd work for you. Every day."

I wanted to tell him to leave. I wanted to tell him to kiss me. I wanted too much and not enough.

My heart hammered, and my voice fell away. I was about a second from caving, giving in completely, when he retreated a step and handed over my clothes.

"I'm not blind, Celia. I can see how I make you feel. I might push you with other stuff, but I won't push you on this. I need you to decide for yourself."

When he walked out and closed the door, I rushed to lean against the sink. I stared at my reflection for a while after, wondering what was holding me back. There was no denying how I'd felt being so close to him. My freckled nose and cheeks were flushed. My eyes were wide and wild, living up to the nickname he liked to torment me with. He could be an ass, a total jerk to get the laughs he wanted, but I knew who he was too. And that was part of it. He was my best friend's brother. It felt weird, like some kind of betrayal, even if Mer and I had never discussed the topic before, deemed him off-limits. Possibly because it was implied or simply not thought of at all.

But maybe I needed to think more about it.

Several minutes later, I moved back into Mer's room, expecting her to be home only to find it empty. As I turned to grab my phone from her bed where I'd left it, I spotted a daisy propped on top of my bag.

13
Celia

-now-

"There you go with that damn phone again," Nadine said with a huff. "I thought you wanted to come out with us tonight?"

"I did. I do. I'm here. Sorry," I admitted, putting down the phone and taking a large gulp of my margarita. Strawberry tonight. Woo.

The girls planned another Friday night drink date with little trouble on schedule coordination. I was happy for it. I needed another distraction. The week had been entirely too long, and I had tried my damnedest to focus on anything else but Caleb and failed. Hard. My mind wouldn't turn him off, replaying the time we'd spent during the weekend, reliving our time in the past, the good and bad mixing all together, weighing me down.

I decided I wouldn't text him first. And so I'd waited, wondering when he'd break the silence, wondering if I was the only one thinking about it all, knowing I shouldn't be thinking about it at all. If anything, at least one good thing had come from honoring Mer's last request. I'd picked up my camera again, even after I finished working during the week. It was another distraction, sure, but also a reawakening of a piece of my soul I'd stupidly allowed to slip away.

Wednesday night it had finally happened. We'd exchanged a few brief texts, choosing the water tower for the next task on Saturday. Thursday had been the same. Short and sweet, asking how my day was, how his day was. And tonight …

"Has he texted you yet?" Nadine asked, snapping my attention back to her. She lifted a perfectly filled eyebrow and pursed her dark stained lips.

I hadn't talked much with her during the week, but she had an uncanny way of knowing things.

"Not tonight," I answered.

"Are you sure he's interested?" Julie jumped into the convo, flashing a pinched and doubtful smile. "I mean, you said he saw Brent at your apartment. I'd be surprised if any guy would be secure enough to try after that."

"Speaking of," Mina interrupted. "Brent seemed to take a lot of trips to your floor this week. Meeting Caleb definitely did something to him. I also didn't see him chatting with his usual down in the claims department or that other one, the newer underwriter with the blond hair and pink Gucci bag."

"That's because he's been jockin' our girl here," Nadine said, wagging those brows and bobble-heading to add some flair.

"Your brows look so good today," I commented before downing some more of my 'rita. "Did I mention that already?"

"Oh thank you, girl. But we're still talking about you. Nice try, though."

Dammit.

"I'm surprised you've noticed much," Deandra said to me, her motherly eyes managing to look both disappointed and angry. "Brent isn't the only one jockin' you. I know Jerry pulled you into his office. You slipped up this week."

"I did. A few honest mistakes. He was pissed."

"You managed to transpose some policy numbers from what his assistant said. That's not good, hon. That's never good," she said with a frown.

"Yeah, I know. I've been out of it all week, thrown off by it all. So, yeah, I'm on notice." Rightfully so. I'd allowed my routine to slip, and I couldn't seem to get things together.

"What a jerk." Julie took a sip on her appletini then grinned wickedly from behind the glass. "I bet a good dicking from Brent would be good for him."

Laughter broke out around the table.

"Well, he can have at it. I've postponed my Brent dicking indefinitely."

"Oh, shit." Mina's eyes popped wide. "So it's not only that he met your Caleb."

Your Caleb. I didn't correct her even though the urge to was at the tip of my tongue. He wasn't mine. And even after both my routine and brain function derailing, I still wasn't sure how I should feel about that. I shouldn't care. But I did.

"He's texted me and stopped at my desk more than usual," I admitted about Brent. "He hasn't come out and asked about Caleb or what might be happening between us, but he knows something's up since I'm fairly predictable and this is the only thing that has changed lately."

"He's scared to lose you. But he should have thought about that shit before he convinced you of the nonexclusive plan, which was mostly about his ability to go dicking around,"

Deandra said. "Men really are the same ol' boys in the sandbox. Don't care about what they're putting down until someone else comes along and snatches it up."

"So true," Mina agreed. "One man's unappreciated chick is another's future queen."

"Tell us about him. Have you …?" Julie asked with a wink and the more obvious sex gesture of stuffing her pointer finger into her closed fist. Nadine reached over and smacked her hands.

"No. We're revisiting the senior year bucket list for Mer and scattering her ashes at all the places. She requested I do the tasks I never completed then leave her at the new locations. So we're reliving some memories and making more, I guess. It's been mostly reflective and kinda sad, but I feel like things might be changing."

"Wow, that is heavy stuff," Julie said.

"Ladies," the bartender from the previous week said, appearing with our next rounds even though he hadn't made the first ones. At least he wasn't late. "How's the list going?"

"What?" I asked, not sure if I'd heard him correctly.

His eyes looked around the table then settled back to mine. "I have to admit I was happy to see you here again when I came on shift. After watching the video about the senior year bucket list you and Merilyn did in high school, I can't stop thinking about it. Is the video right? Is that what you and her brother have been doing in her honor?"

"Oh shit," Nadine murmured. "There's a video? Why do I feel like this is a surprise?"

The bartender smiled at me expectantly.

"What video?" I asked calmly, while my nosy ride-or-dies snatched out their phones and started their research.

"Oh, I thought you would have known." The bartender

frowned. "Like the other wake one. Thinking about it now, it does look a bit sketchy."

"Thanks for the drinks," Nadine said, dismissing him after she noticed my unease. "What's all this about?"

"We're filming it because that's what Mer wanted. It's not getting loaded to her channel until after we're done and the production company edits. That's the info Caleb had. This must be something else, someone else again."

"She had fans, right? People who could have possibly known about the list," Nadine said.

"True. But where—"

"Here it is!" Julie said, holding the phone at the end of the table so we could all watch.

"Oh, girl, that's Caleb?" Mina asked.

"Ooh." The others sighed.

I ignored that bit and watched as the camera zoomed way in to see us standing in the open field where the abandoned house had been torn down. "Shit."

The video was choppy, had no voice-over editing, only pop-up text explaining what we had to be doing. They couldn't even hear what we were saying. It was like some lousy stalker news report. The next clip was of us at Murph's house from a moving viewpoint, the person obviously in a car.

"Damn, Celia. No wonder Brent's all twisted up. Your Caleb is fine," Julie whispered, leaning in closer. "And your ass looks smokin' on camera by the way."

"This is so crappy of someone to do," Deandra commented, her eyes still glued to the phone screen. "You have to tell him and that production company about this. Whoever it is has been following him. Or you!"

"True," I replied, tipping my face down to my phone screen.

Still no message. "I'll text him tonight or tell him tomorrow. They haven't approached us, and it doesn't look like they know what things are on the list, so they won't be able to film much, aside from this crappy style of video. I'm sure the production company Mer worked with will handle it."

"And what about you?" Nadine asked, twisting away from the video to face me.

"What about me?" I gulped down some of the new margarita, the potent, barely diluted tequila making me pucker.

Her long fingers tapped the table, fingernails clicking rhythmically.

When her only other response was to stare at me, I said, "I'm fine. It's fine."

"Something you've been saying quite a lot lately," she noted. "I'm thinking it's not fine."

I shook my head and blurted, "I'm not sure what I'm doing."

"Yes, you do, honey," Deandra said, she and the others abandoning the video and focusing on me. "You know in your heart."

"You also know in your head," Mina added, tapping a finger to her temple.

"And your gut," Nadine said beside me.

Julie looked around at them then back at me with a bite of her bottom lip. "And I'm damn sure you know in your vag." When all eyes and mouths popped wide, she added, "What? He is fucking hot, girl. I might have to change my underwear, and I'm not the one having to stand next to him."

"You nasty," Nadine said as the others burst into giggles.

I tried to stop the smile. I really did. But then it broke free along with a laugh to join theirs. My thoughts were of Caleb, seeing him kiss the cougar, run from the neighborhood watch, talk to the lady in the high school parking lot.

As the laugh died, I released a long sigh. It was nice to day-dream, but reality was still not so simple.

"You'll figure it out," Nadine said.

"Yeah, maybe."

"You have a habit, you know? Of putting things into a specific, very linear order. It's why you're good at your job, most of the time," she added with a smile. "But that's not life. You can't expect it all to stay straight. Things have to change. Things need to change. Otherwise, one day it'll all be over, and the only real memories you've managed to collect are a bunch of could-haves and should-haves."

14
Caleb

-now-

I killed my headlights and used the dim moonlight to guide me the last fifty feet down the water tower's road. I doubted anyone would be around this side of town on a Saturday night anyway, but it was better to be cautious than to get caught by a cop or one of the closer homeowners. Getting arrested because of Mer after her death would be my luck. I also didn't want Celia having to worry. Tonight would be difficult enough.

Her car pulled in behind mine only a few minutes later and it was like I could breathe again.

I'd been so worried during the week, hoping my reaction to the stranger kiss at the arena hadn't scared her off, caused her to change her mind about finishing this. It was why I'd kept the texts between us light. I didn't want to freak her out any more than I already had. Clearly, I had no right to her. I shouldn't have reacted that way at all. But seeing her kiss someone else after we'd spent more time together … I almost couldn't control myself, even with Mer's ashes in hand.

"Hey," I said as she got out of her car and walked to me.

"Hey. Anyone follow you?"

"No, you?" I'd been watching as I drove. When she'd texted me about the video the previous night, I looked it up and determined exactly what she had. Someone had been following us. They didn't have much to go on besides knowing about the list and trying to tag along. I sent an email to the production company with a heads-up, but it was still good to be cautious.

"Nope." Her voice was light as she adjusted the camera bag on her shoulder then smoothed the cream-colored button-down she had on. "I probably should have worn black for this, huh?"

I looked down at my white T-shirt with a laugh. "Yeah, maybe. I hadn't thought about it. At least it's dark."

Coming at night was necessary. Too many eyes were out in the daylight. Waiting another full day to see her had been torture, though.

"And our shirts might blend in with the white paint up there," she said, tipping her face to look high above.

"True," I murmured an agreement, unable to focus on words as I stared at her.

"What?" she asked, catching me.

I shook my head and exhaled with a smile. "I was remembering the night we were here."

"Right," she said with a little nod. "Another one of my failed tasks."

Without thought, I said, "You are as gorgeous as that night, even without your cocoon of winter gear and milkshake perfume."

She inhaled quickly. I'd shocked her. I'd even shocked myself. I wasn't supposed to let it all out while we were doing these tasks. It had to be a bad idea. She was already upset with me. Add on my needy flirtation and she was likely to bolt even faster. But I couldn't help myself as I watched the sliver of moonlight glitter inside those big, soul-stealing eyes. Dammit, I was done for. There was no denying it anymore.

She recovered quickly, shaking her head with a chuckle. "You aren't so bad yourself. And I think I still need to pay you back for those milkshakes."

"Pretty sure you already did. The fair," I noted, recalling the night she'd shocked me in more than one way.

"Oh, right." Her voice was soft.

"But I do deserve way more punishment. I was a shit."

A tiny smile stretched at the corner of her lips, sly and beautiful. I wanted to kiss those lips so badly, devour that sexy smirk.

"So," I said, after clearing my throat to prevent myself from groaning or attempting to act out what was becoming a very vivid situation in my head, "you ready?"

"I think so. Would you be willing to carry the camera bag? I think the urn will fit inside if it makes it easier."

"Of course."

When we got to the ladder, I thought she would hesitate. But she surprised me by jumping right on and starting up. I followed closely behind her, mostly for support, should she have needed it, but also because the view of her ass was spectacular under the glow of a few safety spotlights affixed to the underside of the tower. I was hypnotized by her all over again. The fluid way she moved. The soothing sound of her voice.

"Have you climbed some other water tower I don't know about?" I asked as she slowly and carefully mounted the catwalk.

She took a step forward then sank to her knees, breathing

heavily. "No. I wanted to get it done fast. Cut the preamble, cut the chance of building more fear."

"Smart," I replied. "Congrats. You made it."

"We made it."

"Well, I did do this once already. My senior year."

"Oh. You said you didn't do your own list." She shifted her feet underneath, gripped the railing, and stood.

"Right, not actually a list," I admitted, standing with her. "Others were doing it. Some things were just fun to do. No list needed for me to join in."

"Understandable. Any reason why not, though? Could have been fun."

I glanced up at the moon, watching the clouds move fast across the sky, covering and uncovering the light. "Besides already having done part of one and being occupied with work and football?" I paused, knowing my next words were raw and real and could stir up too much, push too far too fast. "It wasn't the same without you."

The wind picked up, blowing her loose hair forward toward me, strands whirling around her face. "I, uh, should have brought a hair tie."

I stepped closer and reached out, gathering the strands and helping her tuck them back behind her ear and into her shirt collar. The heat of her was intoxicating. The spring night was comfortable even with the heavy wind, but that didn't stop my body from wanting her near, wanting to feel her warmth.

We had a task, though. "You want to get started? I brought the light attachment for the GoPro, but I'd rather not use it. I think it'll ruin the experience, even if the video doesn't show much."

"Okay," she agreed.

When I was ready, I told her, and she began talking. She touched a little on the night we'd been here in the snow, how Merilyn had stayed, fearless and driven. I panned the camera around, taking in the tiny slice of moon as lightning flickered in the distance.

"That's not good," I said with a laugh. "Rain wasn't in the forecast." A rumble of thunder followed.

"Guess it is now. We should probably go. I'm not daring enough to challenge lightning, especially when we're standing on a huge conductor."

I grabbed the urn and handed it over for her to do the honors. As soon as she tipped a small amount over, it disappeared into the night, the wind carrying it off quickly.

"Can I get my camera for a minute? I'd love to get a few quick shots in," she said. "Now I understand why Mer stayed up here so long that night, even in the snow."

"Yeah." It was the only response I could manage as a lump formed in my throat. Emotions were a bitch sometimes, closing a mouth that wanted to speak a thousand words. It was her. It was Mer. All of it.

Her hair escaped its containment and waved out around her again, the ends whipping my face as she steadied her camera onto the rail to set up her shots. I inhaled, needing to capture the moment in my own way, memorizing the fresh water scent that was entirely her and not the approaching storm. House lights blinked in the distance, blotted by the rain.

Another streak of lightning flashed, and thunder was fast to follow, louder and stronger. Celia backed up against me. I instinctively grabbed hold, wrapping my hands around her, dipping my face down alongside her neck.

Her tense body loosened in my arms, and she breathed deeply. "We should go." It was a whisper.

"Yes," I agreed, releasing her then packing her camera.

"I'll go first. That way if you fall, you'll kill both of us." She laughed lightly as I started down the ladder. "No pressure."

"You're such a shit." Another round of thunder followed her words.

She moved a little slower on the way down but made it without killing us both and gave my arm a generous smack right at the bottom.

"We still on tomorrow for the quarry?" I asked, needing re-assurance since it was almost painful having to say goodnight.

"As long as this storm passes, yeah. I have to admit that I'm nervous about that one, though." She took hold of the bag when we reached the cars.

"I'm sure that'll pass as soon as we get there. And I prom-ise not to be as big of an ass as I was then."

"You shouldn't make promises you can't keep." It was likely supposed to be a joke, but it seemed to hit something else as her voice softened and her eyes drifted away.

Damn. A million things were swimming in my head, so many thoughts I wanted her to know. I still felt like it was in bad form to unload it all on her now, to risk the fragile meet-ing place we'd been given. Despite Mer's faults, I wouldn't want to ruin her last request by running Celia off due to my lack of self-control. That had been the cause of many of my problems in the past—no patience, quick action. I needed to wait.

"I hope I haven't been that bad during this to make you feel like I wouldn't."

"No, I'm sorry. I didn't mean it that way." Her words tum-bled out in a whisper.

Following another flash, rain started falling. There was no sprinkle lead-in, only fast, fat drops pounding down to the ground and onto us.

"We better go," I said, feeling the water soak into my hair, my T-shirt, and watching it do the same to her.

"See you tomorrow."

We parted, both retreating to the dryness of our vehicles. I opened my door and set the GoPro and Mer's urn onto the seat. For a moment, my eyes remained locked there on the metal containing my sister's ashes, the biggest regret of my life flashing into my mind. Mer and I were the same in many ways, especially with our rash decisions, over-the-top antics, and drive for adventure. I knew she had her own regrets when she requested Celia and I revisit the list. She knew she'd broken two hearts the night she convinced me to let Celia go. I'd believed Mer's reasoning. If I had followed through with my promise to Celia that night and we'd stayed together, she would have returned every weekend that fall, forgoing lots of experiences, holding her back from the life she deserved to begin.

Given Celia's reserved personality, there had been logic in Mer's argument. Otherwise, I wouldn't have agreed. I wanted what was best for Celia too.

I had no idea what might have happened had I chosen differently. But I knew now that life didn't wait. Things could change. People could die. I was wrong before. Curbing my impulses had been an essential part of growing up, sure. This wasn't the right time for that, though. I needed to stop waiting and stop wasting time.

"Celia!" I yelled, turning around as another streak of lightning lit up the night sky.

She had already started her car, the headlights beaming at me and the back of my truck. When she noticed me walking toward her, she opened her door, stepped out, and yelled, "Something wrong?"

My feet stopped moving halfway between us, all my courage disappearing as I watched the rain thoroughly wet her hair and stream down her gorgeous face. I'd lost all thought staring at her.

A look of alarm crossed over her features. She closed her door and walked right to me, not caring about the rain, about the storm.

"I'm sorry," I said, all other words failing me despite the amount swirling inside my head.

Her eyes squinted and her head tilted. "You already apologized, and I already forgave you."

"Not only for the wake. For everything. For all the times I messed with you. And for never showing up ..." That night.

"Caleb, why are you saying all this now? We can talk tomorrow, okay? It was over a long time ago. But if you need to hear it again tonight, I forgive you."

Without thought, I took one last step closer so my body was flush with hers, palmed her wet cheeks, and lifted her face. I tipped mine down farther, mixing our breaths together. "I've missed you so much. And I know this isn't the perfect time, place, or situation—with the list and Mer and everything else— but I couldn't wait another minute to tell you."

"Why?"

"Because I can't let you go again."

"What about the girl at the wake?"

"That was over the moment you busted into Mer's room," I admitted honestly.

"And there's ... no one else?"

"No. There's never really been anyone else for me. It's always been you."

Her eyebrows knitted together, and she released a breath.

When her brows relaxed, all I could see was the relief in those big fucking eyes, as if she'd been waiting too long to hear those words. And, man, didn't that make me want to go back in time and kick my own ass.

But I wouldn't dwell on that because I had her in my hands, and it was time to live in this moment.

I leaned in and touched my wet lips to hers as the rain continued to fall. Her mouth opened with mine, our tongues meeting gently, like a tentative taste of the sweetest dream, making sure it was real after all. My body surged from the contact, pulsing with so many emotions. Her hands inched up my chest, and I pushed harder, with my tongue, with my mouth, while holding her face as carefully as I could manage. But holy hell I needed to feel more of her.

Dropping my hands and breaking the kiss, I scooped her ass and lifted her body against me. She laughed and braced her forearms on my shoulders while her hands wrapped around the back of my head, fingers curling into my longer strands of hair up top.

"Caleb," she whispered with a smile above my lips.

"Tarsier," I replied, unable to stop myself, enjoying the way she was clinging to me like the adorable little big-eyed primate I'd nicknamed her after.

She released a breathy laugh. "Did you do this on purpose?"

"What?" I asked, closing my eyes for a long moment to focus on the feeling of her in my arms.

Her lips came down to mine, brushing softly.

Fuck. I was overloaded with sensation. Wet clothes. Slick skin. Celia's lips on mine. My hands grasping her ass and thighs. So yeah, my dick strained against my jeans. I stifled a groan.

"This. Kissing in the rain. It was another task I hadn't done."

I smiled. "No, I'd forgotten about that girly shit." We'd seen it when looking over the list at the arena, so she knew I hadn't forgotten. But I hadn't planned it either.

She pinched my lower lip between her teeth—a lovely response to my joke about when we'd started the list—and this time I didn't stifle my groan. Against my mouth, she whispered, "We don't need to film this one."

"Wouldn't dream of it."

Because there was no fucking way I'd share that moment with anyone else.

15
Caleb

-then-

Dipping out of school probably wasn't the best idea, but there were always worse things to get in trouble for. If we got caught, this day would be worth it. Senior skip day. I hadn't planned on partaking. For one, I was a junior, which Mer and Celia both liked to remind me of constantly. And second, well, I wasn't really wanting to get spun up in the hype. But—oh yes, there's a but—when big sister called to say her Corolla broke down, guess who decided to save the day? Especially after finding out skip day would entail a task from the bucket list. My task, to be exact. The one I'd suggested from the start. So you're damn right I'd be there.

And since he was my best friend, Jacob—another junior on the varsity football team—tagged along.

"I'm glad you didn't tell anyone else we were ditchin'," he said, holding his hand out the window and tapping on the roof of The Beast, trying to keep the beat of "Can't Hold Us." He was a bigger guy. Defensive linebacker. Saw a lot of action on and off the field. Couldn't blame the chicks. He was a good guy and good-looking for a dude who'd had his nose broken at least once and went heavy with the hair product to style his way-longer locks up top.

"If you hadn't been standing next to me before the bell, I wouldn't have told you either," I said with a laugh.

He slugged my arm, reaching me easily from the passenger side. "Good thing I'm not as clueless as you, like on the field during a blitz, running back. Wow, this place is a little hike. Where'd they break down? On the Mason-Dixon line?"

"Close. She said it's off the turn before the Maryland border. There," I said, spotting the car pulled over down the gravel access road that led through the woods to the quarry.

Mer and Celia stood outside of the Corolla, which was already jacked up in the back, ready for a tire change. I stared at Celia's bright legs under the strong springtime sun. They glowed and practically sparkled as if they were calling for me.

"Holy shit," Jacob murmured, and I instantly fucking regretted bringing him and thought of ways to ditch him on the side of the road. "Damn, your sister is fine as fuck."

Annnd he could stay.

I shuddered after what he said actually registered, though. Ew.

As I pulled The Beast up behind the Corolla, Jacob whispered in a rush, "She dated Dean for a bit, right? But is she seeing anyone now?"

"I have no clue, man. I'm not about knowing my sister's dating life." Now, about Celia ... She'd gone on another date with Murph the weekend after the water tower, but it didn't continue. Supposedly, she'd also gone out with some guy she'd waited on at The Shack, a senior from our rival school Woodland Prep. A few weeks before, I was happy to overhear her telling Mer that she'd eighty-sixed him after he asked to suck on her feet. I had to give the guy credit for asking. Not that I was into the foot fetish thing, but Celia's were damn cute, and I probably wouldn't say no if she wanted me to kiss 'em.

"Think I've got a shot?"

I side-eyed him as I cranked the stubborn steering column shifter into park.

He shrugged with a laugh then jumped out of the truck with a smile as bright as Celia's legs. "Ladies! Your friendly neighborhood mechanics are here to help."

Mer dropped her sunglasses and scowled at me. "About time."

I shrugged. "Uh, it's over a half-hour drive."

"Do you have a tire iron or not? Someone forgot to put the one in this car back. And why is the bed of your truck stacked with dining room chairs?"

"You didn't tell me you had a flat," I replied, watching Celia avoid looking at me again as Jacob said hi to her. "I have an iron. I'll have to dig. And I was supposed to drop the orders off before school and forgot."

"Dad's gonna have your ass."

"Yeah? Well, guess that'll be two of us when he finds out we both ditched today." I moved to the back and started digging inside the mounted toolbox. Nothing. Not even Dad's ratchet set. I jumped down and went inside the cab, reaching into the small storage area behind the seat. Nada.

"Don't even tell me," Mer said, shaking her head. "Well, most people were going to Murph's house today, but we told a few people our plan. Nobody's passed us, so they might be there already. Just give us a ride. Someone's bound to have a tire iron. We can snatch a ride back here when we leave. You won't need to stick around."

"Ha! Yeah, like staying isn't an option? Get in," I said, climbing behind the wheel.

And whaddya know? There was no room for anyone to jump into the back. Mer and I both would rather her walk than sit next to me. And I'd drop dead before I let Jacob squish up on me. So after they chucked their bags and towels into the bed, Celia climbed in first. Mer was next. Then Jacob managed to squeeze the passenger door shut with the four of us in the seat. It was cozy all right. Jacob was having a hard time hiding his grin as Mer settled in at his side. He ended up tossing his arm over the back of the bench seat so his wide shoulder didn't eat more space, making it even cozier. Mer didn't seem to mind. In fact, she started chatting after I put the truck in gear and took off.

Celia smelled fantastic. She battled to keep most of her body pressed against Mer, but it was impossible. As she shifted her position, her hand pressed onto my thigh. "Sorry."

"Sure you are," I joked, inhaling deeply and clenching all my muscles in an attempt to fight off the semi forming in my pants.

She pursed her pretty lips at me with a shake of her head then tried her best to turn away, her hair spilling onto my shoulder as she readjusted. I had no idea what was happening on the other side of the cab. The chatter wasn't even registering. I was surprised I could even focus on the damn road. She was hypnotizing, and I was enchanted by every move she made.

When we pulled into the quarry, we saw a few other cars parked with people hanging around the cleared grassy space along the edge of the water and the rocky cliff face to the side. The space was open but surrounded by trees and set back far from the main road, keeping it hidden enough that most people weren't even aware of it unless they lived close. There were rumors of a few drowning deaths throughout the years, but there was no fencing or signs to ward off visitors.

"Celia," I said as Jacob and Mer hopped out of the truck.

"Yeah?" She stopped scooting toward the door and glanced back at me.

I had to bite my bottom lip hard. "You look good." Her eyebrows shot up at the compliment. "Hope the jump doesn't wreck you."

"Funny."

The small group of people had been there a while. No one had climbed up to the ledge near the top of the rocky cliff nicknamed Eagle's Nest yet. They said they were waiting a little while for the sun to heat the upper portion of water at least. But with how deep the rock quarry was mined, we all knew it was famous for being cold even on the hottest of summer days. There were about three other girls I didn't know and two other guys. All were interested in hearing more about the bucket list from Mer and Celia.

I hung back by The Beast, barely listening to Jacob talk to me while watching Celia walk around with her camera, taking shots of the trees and the cliffs. It wasn't long before she decided to shed her outer layers, revealing a yellow bikini as bright as her skin. She was a fucking sexy daisy. When I hissed audibly, unable to control my reaction to the dips in her waist, the curve of her ass, and the swell of her breasts, she spun toward me as if she knew.

"Damn, Tarsier, whoever's in space right now is yelling to turn off the light," I joked to cover my slip.

Jacob laughed beside me and others joined in, including Mer, who added, "You are in serious need of the sun, babe."

Celia rolled her eyes at me then turned to Mer. "I can't disagree with that. That's why I'm here."

"Oh, no, you aren't." I pushed away from the truck and walked over to the group, standing beside their row of towels and bodies. "You're here for the bucket list, not to lie out or compete with the sun for the title of who blinds the most eyes. I'm ready to see you jump."

Celia glared at me while the others began to chant. "Jump. Jump. Jump."

"Me first," Mer said, bouncing up onto her feet and stripping down to her suit.

Jacob was fast to follow her, kicking out of his shoes and wrenching off his shirt, leaving a trail of clothes behind him as he went.

There was chatter from the others about it being too cold yet and blah, blah, blah. I wasn't listening. I was in a stare down with Celia, who finally caved and walked off toward the bottom edge of the cliff where the climb started. I followed her, kicking off my gear like Jacob had, stripping down to my boxer briefs since I didn't have my board shorts.

"You couldn't let me relax, could you?" Celia said as she navigated the narrow path that began to increase in height, skirting behind the base boulders jutting out from the cliff face.

I quickened my pace until I was right behind her, watching every one of her careful steps. She still had her camera slung around her neck and had pulled her mass of long hair up into a loose, messy bun at the crest of her head with pieces escaping at the edges of her face, creating a wild and sexy sort of frame. She glanced back at me when I hadn't replied.

"What can I say? I live to mix up your perfectly sorted crayons."

She released a breath that was part huff part chuckle, sounding aggravated yet mildly amused. "Of course you do." Her footsteps slowed as she shimmied around a large boulder, gripping the limestone hard, as if her feet weren't on the ground.

"Are you afraid?" I asked, honestly curious.

"To jump? No."

"Then why are you on edge about it?"

"The jump and the fall aren't what scare me. That part is fun. But when that rush ends ... there's a crash at the bottom. If it never ended, it wouldn't be an issue. But everything has to end, right?"

"Wow, Tarsier, that's some deep shit right there."

"Where are you, Celia?" Mer's voice shouted from above. Her lifted arms and face came into view after we moved around a twist in the cliff's tiny pathway. "There you are! C'mon!"

When Celia didn't say anything else, I asked, "So that's why you stay in the lines a lot, huh? It's comfortable there, no crash to worry about?"

"I guess," she replied, breathing heavily as she peeked out over the cliff.

I bolted ahead of her, climbing around a few bushes and over one last boulder onto the flat of Eagle's Nest where Jacob and Mer stood at the edge, waving out to the others below. Looking down at Celia, watching her focus as she tilted her camera up the last bit to take a picture of Mer was like being hit with something profound. And no, it wasn't only her beauty—though she looked more beautiful, and sexier than ever—but something more I realized. I didn't just want her. I craved more of her and the calmness she seemed to bring me from being close, like nothing else mattered.

She turned, and I reached out a hand to help her with the

final step up. Her eyes narrowed with doubt, wondering what I might do, but then she slipped her soft palm into mine, letting me take hold. With my feet planted, I pulled as she took a step, her body coming flush to mine. I didn't back off. I needed a moment with her close. And she didn't object like I thought she might. She merely tipped those eyes up to me and parted her lips—

"Yes! I can't wait anymore," Mer said with a laugh, jumping over to us, tugging Celia away. "I'm going first. Take my picture?"

"Yeah," Celia agreed, moving to the edge, not looking back. She waited, watching Mer sprint forward and launch herself into the air.

As Celia snapped several pictures, I joined Jacob, tracking Mer's fifty-foot free fall and splash into the dark blue water.

"I'm up," Jacob said.

"You sure, man? You don't have any backup hair shit," I joked, with my eyes still pinned on Celia, who waved to Mer below. "Get ready to capture a magical oil-slick rainbow inside the water after Jacob goes in, Celia."

Jacob backed up as far as the cliff allowed. "I might leave you more than that to jump into, asshole."

"Don't you piss down there!" I said as he ran by. He slugged my arm as he went then threw himself off with a "Wooooooo!"

Celia laughed behind her camera, capturing Jacob's epic cannonball from high above.

I snuck up behind her, grabbed her around the waist, and yanked her backward instead of pushing. She screeched then spun around, crazy eyed and ready to fight.

Releasing her and holding up my hands, I said, "Joke. I wouldn't do that from this high."

Her breaths were quick, her cheeks flushed. "Dammit, Caleb."

I grabbed the camera, lifting the strap over her head and clicking a few shots of her as she calmed down. "Jump with me."

"What? No. I have my camera. It's not waterproof."

"I'll come back up and get it. Come on, Celia. Let's fall together." I set her camera down, stepped in close, and ran the tip of my fingers along her jaw. "I promise I'll be there after the crash." She knew I wanted more, that this wasn't only about the jump. I needed her to be mine.

For a few moments, she was silent, and I let myself think that maybe …

"I can't. I just can't."

Ouch. Fucking hell, the rejection hurt worse every time. I wanted to ask her why, demand a valid reason. But I took the hit as I had before, knowing that despite all the times I'd vowed to stop asking, there'd likely be another next time.

"Right," I said, backing away. "Be careful on the way down, okay?"

Because I had no plan to stick around the rest of the day torturing myself.

I smiled at her then took the jump, already feeling the crash.

Celia

-now-

Caleb's place sat on a dairy farm owned by a Mennonite family at the south-western border of Ellville. It was a square cottage-style house with white siding, fixed black shutters, and a small front porch big enough to hold two wooden rockers and a tiny table—no doubt he'd handmade himself.

After leaving the water tower the night before, he'd insisted I meet him at his place to take the rest of the drive to the quarry together. What he'd offered to do was drive all the way to pick me up even though it would have been a huge waste of travel and time for him, so we compromised. In reality, I barely cared how we managed to get together. Walk, run, crawl on all fours—I was prepared to do anything to see him. The previous night had been amazing. His words had erased my concerns and had me melting inside his arms. And the kiss we'd shared … Yeah, I had to force myself back into my car when all I really wanted was to stay right there with him in the storm, lightning be damned.

"Hi," he said, coming out of his house to meet me. He slung a backpack and a towel over his shoulder then picked up a cooler from the porch.

"Hi," I replied, locking my car while watching him load the cooler into the back seat of his truck.

"Did you want to see my place before we leave?" he asked, twisting his keys in hand.

I stared at the cute house, knowing how bad of an idea that was.

He laughed lightly and bit his bottom lip, knowing exactly what I was thinking. Shit. "Probably best we get to the quarry."

"Yeah," I agreed, stepping up to the passenger door where he met me.

"Come here," he whispered, lifting his hands to my cheeks and staring into my eyes. "I've been waiting all night and morning to taste these lips again."

"It was a long time," I admitted.

"So long." He took my mouth fully, sliding his tongue in to meet mine smoothly, passionately. The scruff along his jaw and upper lip rubbed against my skin, prickling.

The intensity made me feel weak. I clenched the sides of his T-shirt, needing to stabilize.

He eased off, kissing me once more chastely then smiling against my lips. "We should leave."

"Yes," I replied with my own smile.

He released my face then opened the passenger door for me before jogging around the front of the truck. Right away, the woodsy smell of sawdust hit me—cedar and pine and whatever else. The floor mats were clean but still had traces of it along the edging. His center console storage area was lifted, the urn and the bucket list notebook standing upright inside.

"What?" he asked when he hopped in and started the engine, eyeing me curiously.

"Just smells exactly like The Beast did. Like you. Like sawdust."

He exhaled a laugh and pulled away from the house with a smile bigger than my own. His hand reached around the center console, past the urn and notebook, his palm twisting up. I slid mine over it, and he instantly threaded our fingers.

"Glad you brought a bag to change. Did you eat lunch already?"

"I did."

"Okay. And no one followed you?"

"No. What did the production company have to say?"

"They found the video and got it taken down like the one from the wake. It was a newer anonymous account. They think it might be one of their old crew members who was close with Mer. They said not to worry too much but to report if anything else happens."

"Good to know. Hopefully nothing does." Not wanting to dwell on that, I asked, "So you rent from the farm owners? How do you like it?"

His fingers moved inside my grasp, sliding back and forth like he needed to feel more, touch more. "I like it. The cow smell isn't as bad since I'm over the hill from the main grazing field and barn. They have daily pickups at four in the morning, though." He laughed when I grimaced. "Every day except Sundays, of course. I'm used to it, so I don't mind. The rent is reasonable, and it's close to the warehouse."

"It looked nice. Peaceful there."

"The owner, Eli, inherited it from his family. He and his wife are in their thirties and have two daughters under ten. So if he needs quick help with anything when his workers are off, I give him a hand. Mer saw the place during a visit last year after I moved in. She said it was the last thing she pictured for me, stuck here, living on a farm, and especially that I was back working for Dad. But I've always loved the job, and I want to help him grow the company. It was an easy decision. I'm happy with it."

"I can picture you there, pushing those cows around," I admitted while actually picturing him shirtless and sweaty, carrying bales of hay, hosing himself off on a hot summer day. Heat rushed through me.

"I've always had a knack for being pushy."

"You do. And persuasive. Perfect for that business degree. And if you decided to quit the woodworking biz, I'm sure those cows wouldn't mind having you as a manager."

"I'm sure they'd be impressed with my skills." He flashed a sly smile my way before focusing back on the road. "What about you? Are you happy, Celia?"

Hmm. "I suppose I am."

"That doesn't sound very convincing."

"Well, I have a decent job. My apartment is nice. It's not perfect, but what really is?"

"Living where you want to. Having a job or career that you love, that makes you happy. Or working toward a goal for those things. That's close to perfection."

"True."

"So why not leave your job and do what you love?" His hand squeezed mine while he jerked his chin toward my camera bag.

"I'm not sure. I guess I'm comfortable at Pearson Insurance and haven't thought much about leaving."

"Ah. Do they at least treat you well? Give you advancement options?"

I laughed, thinking of Jerky Jerry and my stagnant, practically entry-level position. "Not really, no."

"It's not because of … the coworker guy that was at your place?"

"Oh! No, nothing to do with him. In fact, that won't happen anymore. Him, I mean. He won't happen anymore," I said in a rush, wanting to kick myself immediately after. Was telling him that my time with Brent was over being too presumptuous? Or was it better to say so, as he had told me about the girl at the wake the previous night? It had been a while since I'd been exclusive with someone. And was I assuming that Caleb wanted something on that level with me? *Stop. Just stop thinking.*

"Really? Hope I'm not the reason. I mean, he seemed like a great guy when I met him. Super nice." He smirked to the windshield with a devilish pull of his lips.

My mouth popped open. "You are such an—"

"Ass. I know. I've been called that a time or two thousand."

"One thousand and ninety of them came from Mer."

He laughed, full and deep and so sexy. I wanted to join him, but I was too mesmerized by the sound. It had been an eternity since I'd heard it so loose and carefree. Now it was richer and more resonant, the tone reaching more places than my ears. I inhaled deeply to keep my thoughts and body in check.

"Shit, it's so true. She handed me mine so many times."

"Me too."

"Yeah, that was when she wanted to mother you like you were her baby bird, so frail and innocent."

"Shut up. She didn't."

"That's probably the most bogus statement I've ever heard from you, not that you told me many. Though, there was that one time you tried to convince me that eye masks could help retain study information better."

"Um, pretty sure I did convince you of that."

"No," he said, shaking his head.

"But you took mine and wore it all the time."

"Oh, yes, I wore it." He lifted his eyebrows with a glance at me. "I had some sweet dreams too."

Oh! My cheeks were on fire. "All right, maybe Mer did mother me," I admitted, moving back to the point.

"Yeah, she wanted to push you but never really followed through. That's why she was a better friend than me. I couldn't seem to stay behind those lines."

"Pushy," I replied with a small smile. "She helped me in many ways, though. Was always there for me then."

"I know." His voice softened.

He kept hold of my hand the last few minutes. We were both content in silence, thinking about Mer, about the past.

When we pulled down the gravel road to the quarry, a few cars were already parked in the makeshift lot. The area mostly looked the same. Some trees had grown a little taller and fuller, their lush canopy shading the back portion nicely.

"Is that a cabin at the far end?" I asked, staring at the massive two-story building with a double deck and a fire pit close to the water.

"I heard the property was sold, but I had no idea they built on the land. Looks like a lodge or something. There's another access road too."

Driving in farther, we noticed more space had been cleared for vehicles, the road extending out and around the cabin.

Caleb parked, and we jumped out. Past the line of trees, a few people lounged on the water's edge on a tiny strip of sand.

"They made a little beach."

"Look," Caleb said, moving toward a bench beside a small wooden building labeled restrooms. Signs were posted, warning swimmers of various hazards and asking to pick up their trash. "Guess they adapted for visitors. You ready to do this?" His hand slipped under my hair to grasp the back of my neck. His touch was reassuring but my nerves started ramping up.

"As I'll ever be."

We stripped down to our swimsuits. I tried not to think about how cold the water likely was, but its icy assault when swimming on senior skip day was hard to forget. I found Caleb's eyes on me as I turned, lids low and lusty. The look was enough to melt all my icy thoughts.

"The memories … I half expected you to be in a bright yellow bikini. And I see that skin of yours is still competing with the sun."

With a shake of my head, I chuckled, recalling it all too. Then I stared at him, his bare chest solid with even more pronounced grooves and ridges in his abs than he'd had back then. His skin was already golden tan, some of it natural, some possibly from soaking up the spring sunshine. The V-cut that disappeared into his mint green board shorts didn't go unnoticed either. And a tattoo on his shoulder, with a thick central base and spindly lines that forked and curled intricately up and down, branching out.

"Alder tree," he said. "Celtic astrology."

"You always did have a strong connection with that piece of your heritage. And trees, of course. Is that your only one?"

He nodded.

"I guess I'll be getting my first soon enough. I also need to lie out and spend more time in the gym apparently." I looked down at my belly pooch and doughy office muscles.

"No chance. You couldn't be more perfect," he said, those eyes boring their heat into me again. After a few quick blinks, he handed over the GoPro and a towel, slinging his own over a shoulder. "I don't want to take the urn to the top." He reached into the cabin and looked around for a moment then reemerged and locked up. After unscrewing the urn, he unfolded a tissue in his hand and poured some of Mer's ashes into it. "She's going to jump again with us."

My heart felt fuller than it had in so long as I watched him hold the small pile, twist the tissue to secure it, then close his fist tightly.

We dropped our towels at the edge of the cliff alongside the sandy area. Some people were hanging out there. A few more floated in the water.

With the GoPro recording the climb and the view, I pointed toward the lodge. "Check it out."

The building was lovely to look at. Behind the second floor deck, a wall of windows stretched to the cathedral roof and down to the first deck too. It had to be open inside. Maybe a lobby or even a dining space. There was no seeing past the sun's reflection to know for sure. Smaller windows lined the other sides on both floors, obviously rooms. A few tiny cabins sat farther beyond, tucked into the surrounding trees and mimicking the look of the lodge.

Laughter traveled down from above. There were others up top.

Caleb crested the last section and turned to offer me his free hand. I felt as if I'd stepped right into the past. He grinned, knowing exactly what he was doing.

"Smooth."

"I know."

"Yo!" Teens were standing on the flat of Eagle's Nest—two guys, two girls—watching us. One of the guys had given the greeting.

Caleb tilted his chin. "Hey, man." He released my hand, and I moved around the space, filming the view from the top and over the edge.

"Y'all filming for a vlog?" the same guy asked.

"Wait!" A girl in a purple one-piece spoke up, pointing a finger. "Do I know you from—Oh! You were on the video about the Adventure Life chick, right?"

Crap. Caleb started to shake his head, ready to deny it, but the others joined in with their own recognition.

And the two girls … well, their eyes were practically popping from their heads as they stared at him.

I gritted my teeth and swung the GoPro around, calming my breaths. He wasn't technically mine. And if they were eighteen … he was twenty-two. Not a huge difference. My heart pounded wild and angry at the thought.

"We kinda hoped to have some privacy up here for this," Caleb said, glancing down at his closed hand. "You all staying up here or jumping?"

When I spun around, I caught the two guys eyeing me. *Oh.* I looked over at Caleb again and noticed his jaw clench. Well, all of this was interesting and a little awkward.

"We're jumping, yeah. You want to record us?"

"Sure, if you're agreeing to be filmed," Caleb agreed. "Just don't die. You eighteen?"

The girls answered first, both squeaking out a "Yes" followed by the specifics of their actual birthdays.

Caleb didn't respond only waited for the guys to admit the same then walked over behind me, brushing my hair over my shoulder, fingertips skimming my skin as light as a feather. "Okay, she'll film your jumps. Go for it."

"All right. Bet." The first took a few steps back then ran for the edge. I tracked his launch and then his entry. The girls went next, holding hands with a small jump, squealing all the way down. The last guy sprinted the few yards to the edge and dove straight out before tucking into a flip.

"Wow," I murmured.

"Showoff," Caleb said right next to my ear.

"You jealous of his skills? Really? He's probably here every weekend."

"No. Only jealous that he had your attention at all."

I turned, letting the camera fall to my side. "I'm not sure if I can do this." It all had hit me suddenly. I didn't just mean the jump, and he knew it. My life was simple. At least it had been up until Mer's wake. Everything had changed again in a rush. Now I was worried about him, about other girls around him, about where we both lived, the distance.

"You told me the fall didn't scare you, only the crash. I'm here. I'm not going away."

I cringed, thinking about how he hadn't been there that one night years before. He'd disappeared. "How can I believe that when you never told me why you weren't there? I never got a reason, Caleb. I want to forgive you, badly, but I can't help feeling this way. It hurt. You hurt me. Worse than anyone ever had."

"Celia," he said, palming my cheeks and lifting my face gently. His thumb brushed under my eyes, wiping my frustrated tears away. Dammit. "There was so much I couldn't say then. So much happening with me, too. With school, work, and football. Preparing for my own senior year. I was stupid and angry, and I chose to listen to someone instead of deciding myself."

"What are you talking about?"

He shook his head the slightest bit and licked his lips. "I don't think it's a good idea to—"

"Nope, don't you dare back out of this. I deserve to know."

"I made the choice. It was my choice. But. Shit. Mer knew how close we were getting and she was worried that I would hold you back."

"What? That's ridiculous."

He inhaled deeply and released a long breath. "She told me that if we stayed together, you would've come home every weekend when fall semester started, you would've been back here with me instead of experiencing the college life. She said she loved you too much to let that happen, said that you needed to get away as much as she did."

"I ... that's ..."

"I made a mistake. It's one I regretted that very same night, and ever since."

"I thought you didn't want me. That maybe you were laughing at me. Like I'd been some joke to mess with one final time."

"No, never. Shit, I really should have told you. Even months later, I should have. But I knew you hated me after that, and I couldn't bring myself to approach you again, to tell you the truth—that I am an ass, one who thought he was doing the right thing at the time." His face dipped farther, pressing his forehead to mine. "I was so wrong."

"If that was the case, then it was my choice to make. Not Mer's. Not yours. Mine." I pulled away and crossed my arms over my chest even though I was already struggling for a decent breath of air. I'd been so wrong about it all.

"I should have let you make it, and I understand if you can't forgive me for that. But if you give me another chance to make it right, make it up to you, I'll take whatever punishment you see fit, no question. Want to call me an ass every day, forever? Sure. Stare relentlessly at me with those deadly eyes? Okay. Blind me with your bright skin? I'll take any and all of it."

Closing my eyes, I drew in a calm breath. I'd been upset by it all for so long that it felt good to know an actual reason, the entire truth, and to feel like I could finally let it all go. Perhaps I would still mourn the time that we could have had together, but I needed to focus on the future and starting a new routine, one that allowed breaks in my linear path.

I opened my eyes to his light browns, a mix of worry and wonder stirring inside them as they watched me attentively.

"I'm ready for the fall."

17
Caleb

-now-

“Thank fuck.”

She laughed sweetly.

“Shit. I said that out loud, huh?” I asked, and she nodded while biting her lower lip. “Well, I’m relieved. So damn relieved. I’m not sure what I would have done if you shot me down again up here. Jumped off and left like the last time, I suppose. Go home, ground myself since no one else will, eat a half-gallon of rocky road—”

“You did not,” she said, eyes wide.

“Oh, yes, I did. My mom was more pissed about that than ditch day. I can still hear her yelling, and I quote, ‘Dammit, Caleb! There better be a new one in the freezer tomorrow.’”

“That’s her favorite, right? I’m surprised you lived.”

“Barely.” And it felt close to the truth, only not by my mom’s hand. My heart had almost given up.

“You never told me. Even when we got together, you never told me that you’d felt so … strongly.”

“I had to guard myself a little, Tarsier,” I admitted, breaking out her nickname now, feeling closer than ever. Man, did it feel good. "You crushed me so many times. I wasn't sure how much more I could take. I was crazy for you, probably even bordered the wack job line, though I never crossed it. Don't get me wrong, I thought about it, thought about all the things I wanted with you, so many things."

Her fingertips were soft as they reached up and trailed along my jaw and cheek. "I thought about you, too. So much." She pushed up onto her toes, beckoned my face down, then pressed her lips to mine, propping the GoPro onto my shoulder.

I snaked my arms around her back, splaying my empty hand across her smooth skin then down to the top edge of her bikini bottom, holding her closer. It was real. All of it. Though I had a difficult time convincing myself. It felt as if I'd imagined it all since the night before, since I'd kissed her at the water tower in the thick of the storm. I had to lift her body to mine then, afraid she'd disappear like she had so many times in my dreams.

"Yo!" a shout in the distance brought my mind back to the present. That dude was calling from down below somewhere.

Even though I didn't want to stop kissing Celia, I realized that we still had a task to complete. The reason we were standing fifty feet above the quarry water.

"Mmm," she hummed against my lips when I started to pull away.

"Yeah," I whispered, agreeing with how good it felt. "More later. Way more. You will have to tell me to stop kissing these lips."

"I doubt I'll ever tell you that." She eased away from me, moved to the cliff edge, and held out the GoPro, checking the settings.

When I stepped to her side, I saw the guy and his friends

near the start of the climbing path, out of the water. They were waiting to see us jump.

"Crap, I didn't hit stop," Celia said, eyes still on the tiny camera screen. "All of that recorded."

"Huh. That should make for some interesting editing. We can do it ourselves later if you want."

"Yeah, that's probably best. Are you ready?"

"Yes, let's do this." When she waved her hand, I started talking.

The goofy smile I was sportin' refused to leave my face. As much as I tried to focus on the reason we were here and the intrinsic sadness death brought, and the fact that our previous footage had been more on the somber side, there was no denying that this task was going to be wildly different. Mainly because jumping from a cliff was straight up fun. And also, I was happy, and there was no way I could dim that shit. So instead, I embraced it, explaining not only the tasks that had been completed here back in high school and what Celia needed to do today, but also telling Mer's followers how excited she would have been to be here again, and how being happy and living life was what she would have wanted. They didn't need to know that my happiness had to do with Celia. What counted was that I knew Mer would be excited for this moment, seeing us together again, celebrating her together.

"So we're going to jump, and she'll join us," I said, holding up a tissue then joking, "I can practically hear her yelling at me now about this tissue, though. She probably would have demanded a confetti cannon or something, even with the jump." Celia laughed, tilting the GoPro up and down, nodding in agreement. "Celia, do you want to hold Mer or the camera?"

"It might be best for you to hold the GoPro because I might drop it in the water."

I switched out with her. After taking the camera, I opened the tissue and settled the ashes into her palm, then tucked the tissue into my pocket. Knowing she was nervous, I closed her fingers around the ashes and looked right into her eyes. "You want to go together?"

"Yes, please."

"Okay." I dropped the GoPro to my side for a moment and kissed her, hoping it would help calm her. Snagging her free hand, I threaded our fingers and backed away from her lips. "Let's do it. I'll have to let go after we jump to be safe. Look straight so you don't lean forward or backward. And keep your legs together before going in."

As we stepped up to the edge, her hand shook and her toes wiggled against the rocky lip.

"On three?" I asked, and she nodded. I held out the GoPro facing us and squeezed her hand in mine. "One. Two. Three!"

We leapt forward. Letting go of her hand, I spun and angled the camera toward her. She screamed and opened her hand to the sky, releasing Mer. There were a few cheers following our fall, meeting us from below as we plunged into the cold water.

I kicked and broke through the surface as fast as I could, swimming for where Celia had landed. She burst through right after, gasping a breath before revealing a huge smile with a laugh that put my favorite things in life to shame. Tacos. Sleeping in on the weekends. Working a fresh piece of cedar on a lathe. Maybe even … nope, not sex. But it was damn close.

"That was incredible!" she said, wiping the water from her face with one hand as the other continued to tread below the surface.

More cheering came from the little strip of sand. The

group that had jumped before us waved then disappeared into the parking area.

"Come here." Wrapping my free arm around her back, I took her lips with mine. Our legs worked below, keeping us afloat while we moved together, our tongues swirling sweetly. I moaned as energy and excitement coursed through me, desire building with each stroke of her tongue, each slide of her skin against mine. Recalling the GoPro, I broke away and switched it off. "You did amazing."

"Did I?" she asked. "I probably had the most horrific look on my face. I was so afraid I'd close my eyes, I purposely opened them wider."

The thought of how she looked, how she felt against me—it all made one more thing stir below the surface. "You were … hideous," I said as seriously as I could while trying my best to keep my thoughts in check, which was damn hard to do. "I mean, the smile on your face alone was repulsive. And don't get me started on your eyes. The excitement in them made me a little nauseous."

Her hand darted out, splashing me in the face.

And the battle was on.

She saw the intent in my delighted expression, twisted around with a little scream, and swam furiously toward the edge of the water by the parking area. I gave chase, struggling to catch her with the GoPro in hand. But when I did, a second before she reached the water's edge, I spun her around, slipped my arms beneath hers, and grabbed hold of the rocky ledge to support us both. For a moment, I remained still, allowing our rushed breaths to mingle while staring into her wild, exhilarated eyes. Fuck. The moment should have happened so long ago. There was no reason to think about that, though. She was with me, here and now, ready to move forward with a kiss, and maybe so much more.

I kissed her. I kissed the ever-loving shit out of her. Not willing to waste a single second. I was truthful when I'd said she would have to tell me to stop kissing her. I wanted to keep going forever.

After many more chases, plenty of kisses, and even one more jump from Eagle's Nest, we finally left the water. The sun had dipped behind the treetops, the air cooling in its absence. I dropped my tailgate and grabbed the cooler, breaking out the water bottles and the food I'd packed.

"Wow. I'm impressed," Celia said, unwrapping her pb&j. She took a big bite then tipped her face to soak in the final rays of sunlight.

"Hey, now," I mumbled around my bite before swallowing. "Don't be hating on pb&j. It knows it's not the cheese and champagne picnic you and this day deserve, but it'll do its best to be good fuel for our bodies."

She licked some peanut butter from her finger, her tongue making a slow stroke before taking the tip into her mouth fully. Fuck me. The sight was even more erotic because it was unintentional. I swallowed thickly. Her eyes caught my stare, and she flashed a tiny smile. "Aw. I love pb&j. I just thought I'd grab something on the way home. But thank you for this. It is hitting the spot right now."

"You know …" I hopped down from the tailgate and moved to the cab, snatching the notebook and flipping it open when I got to her. "There are more tasks we need to do." I popped a few grapes into my mouth, waiting for a reaction.

"Yeah?" Her eyes narrowed.

"Stay with me tonight?" I slid my hand over her thigh and squeezed lightly.

"What?" she asked with a laugh. "Stay? It's Sunday night. I have to work tomorrow. We can do more next weekend."

"I know, but hear me out. We can check off a few more things here and now. Sleep under the stars. Watch the sunrise."

"So you want to stay out here tonight?"

"Yes."

"We don't have a tent or any gear."

"That's what makes spontaneity fun, Tarsier." I winked at her, and she pursed her lips. "Okay, I get it. The idea might be a little too thin on details and enticements. Hang on a minute." I was off at a sprint but hadn't thought it through. Because while I had my wallet in my pocket, my feet were still very bare.

She called after me, "Caleb! Where are you—" And then she started laughing as I hopped from one foot to the other, my run faltering as the rocks beneath my soles dug into my tender skin like tiny battle swords.

"Ow. Shit. Fuck. Damn. Ooh. Ow." I kept jogging, though, making my way up to the lodge. I paid no attention to the entry or the decor. I only wanted one thing. Okay, actually a few things. Soft and fluffy and comfy things. And maybe some fucking Band-Aids.

The older lady at the reception desk informed me that Shadywood Lodge was fully booked, having a few families in the tiny cabins and a writing retreat in the main lodge. She emphasized the latter by pointing to the lobby seating area where several women were lounging on plush leather seats by the fireplace, laptops open and headphones on. A few looked up at me and may have stared a bit longer than necessary, which gave me an idea. I put on my best smolder face and asked the receptionist my questions, but that didn't work. I also tried the professional approach, offering my business card and a set of custom lobby chairs. No dice. Finally, after some small talk about the lodge and about Lucy's pet cat named Ethel, who recently had a run-in with a horny skunk, I ended up paying the cost of a night stay, even though we wouldn't technically be sleeping under any of their roofs. A little while later, I was out the door with two thin blankets, two pillows, and a thick comforter all bundled in my arms.

I didn't run again. No way.

The parking area was mostly empty when I returned. Only two cars were parked at the back, the chilly air and setting sun scaring everyone away. Before I reached the truck, a blue car started and drove over to the main parking lot behind the lodge. That left a black coupe, which looked to be owned by a couple who were packing up their stuff on the strip of sand. *Ah.* Solitude was ours.

"You can't be serious with that." Celia said from somewhere around the stack of comfy fluff in my arms.

I twisted my body to the side, still taking care of where I stepped while I looked at her. "As serious as you tried to be when you gave me your eye mask."

"Caleb, I have to be at work in the morning. I don't think this is a good idea," she said, covering her mouth with a hand.

I finally got to the truck and dumped the bundle of comfort into the bed. "I'll set my phone alarm. I'll drive you all the way to your place. You should have about an hour or so to shower and get to work."

"I won't have my car."

"I'll take you to your car first then, and if you want me to, I'll follow you to your place to be sure you get there safe."

She took an incredibly deep breath and let out a sigh behind her hand. Her eyes flitted around, considering my idea, the area. "All right." The words were a tentative whisper.

"What? What was that?" I asked, grabbing her thighs and turning her toward me. Her legs dropped over the tailgate, and I stepped between them. "I didn't hear you."

She let her hand fall, revealing a shy and sexy smile stretching her lips. "I said all right. I'll stay."

Celia

-then-

The lights at the fair had always been my favorite thing about it. Bright and twinkling. Magical and fantastical. The people came in at a close second. Wondrous eyes. Adventurous, thrill-seeking energy—or for kids, sugary, cotton candy energy. And of course there were all the amorous glances, words, and touches. Love, in so many variations, was everywhere at the fair. Even beside me at the ticket booth.

"Why the fair, though?" Jacob asked Mer after buying their tickets. "Hershey Park is always good. Stable. And the odds of the Ferris wheel falling apart while we're on it and decapitating tons of people is far less than at a county pop-up fair."

I cringed at his rather gruesome depiction while I strapped on my neon yellow, all-rides band. At least I wasn't planning to ride the Ferris wheel like they were, so there was a chance my more pleasant views of the fair would remain intact. Along with my head, apparently.

"Because we've all been to Hershey a million times," Mer said, tying up her golden hair and stepping aside for the next

J.M. MILLER

person in line at the booth. "I love it, don't get me wrong, but a fair is different. And lots of fun for many other reasons. So we're taking our chances with a guillotine wheel because our kiss at the top will be another check off the bucket list!"

Mer and Jacob hadn't seemed exactly right together initially. He was more precise with life in general, especially his hair. And she … wasn't. But they'd hooked up shortly after the quarry trip and had been on a few dates since.

Tonight, I was playing third wheel. I didn't mind so much. We were supposed to meet up with some others. I'd also brought my camera and planned to take several shots to add to my portfolio for school and other submissions.

"Okay, ready?" Mer said, tugging on my arm.

I nodded, and she bolted forward into a jog. My camera bag flapped at my back as Jacob's voice yelled from somewhere behind us, "Hey, wait up!"

It was a dash to the big wheel, dodging meandering bodies carrying massive bags of popcorn, and kids on the run to either the impossible games or the porta-potties. When we stopped in the line, I looked up in awe at the lights and the endless night beyond.

"You're going on, right?" Mer asked, tipping her head back too.

"Nah."

"Why not? You might get paired with someone, you know?" Her elbow knocked into my arm a couple of not-so-subtle times.

"Not taking that chance, thanks. I'd rather skip it for now. Maybe I'll end up going to Hershey one day to mark this one off the list."

"Or you could wait for the others to show. Jacob said a lot of the team would be here tonight."

It was funny that the only football teammate I seemed to think of was Caleb even though I didn't think of him as a footballer much. But he had been on my mind a lot more. After the trip to the quarry, he was always MIA whenever I was at their house. According to Mer, he'd taken on extra hours with his dad at work and was spending more time with friends. I couldn't help but be a little sad every time I expected him to bust into Mer's room or show up in random places. I hadn't even seen him at school or for his birthday. I'd honestly missed him. His quippy humor. His incessant taunting. His soulful eyes. His big ears. His sexy smile.

Shit.

"You all right?" Mer said right before Jacob walked up behind us, his usual musky scented cologne hitting my nose before he even spoke. It wasn't bad. Just not what I liked. I preferred woodsy. Like the freshly cut type. Go figure.

"Fine. I'm fine. It's fine. You guys go. Knock out the next task." I pointed up to the top bucket. "I'm gonna walk around and get some shots."

Mer leaned into me with a hug and smashed a kiss to my cheek. "Thank you, babe. Love you." When she pulled away, she flashed her playful smile then turned to Jacob and pushed him forward with her.

I waited there until they hopped into their orange bucket then backed up more and pulled out my camera. They worked, those two. One, a seemingly more straight-laced junior with his shit together. The other, as crazy and adventurous as she always was. They'd already made plans for prom the following weekend.

Mer waved her arms around as the wheel moved them up, stopping a few times to load more passengers.

"Hey," a familiar voice said from behind me.

I turned around and came face-to-face with Murph. A few other football guys and cheerleaders Elise and Marie were laughing and joking close behind him.

"Hey," I replied, looking into his easy eyes.

"So, I know we haven't talked in a while, but I was wondering if—"

"Do it. Do it. Do it," the guys had overheard his words and started to chant, drawing some attention.

Flustered by what I was almost positive was going to be a promposal, I averted my eyes, trying to think of what to say. I liked Murph. He was good-looking, with warm tawny skin, gentle eyes, and a brilliant smile. Kind. Nice. Smart. Check. Check. Check. Also, a decent kisser. He was fine. Fine, as in okay fine. And that was why I hadn't gone on more dates with him. He might be perfect for someone else, but he was merely okay fine to me. And I realized that fine wasn't good enough.

While they continued a chant and Murph turned to them, telling them all to fuck off in a calm mumble, I looked behind them and saw someone who was way more than fine for me.

Caleb walked with another friend toward the haunted house entrance. His hair had been recently cut, shaved closer on the sides with shorter golden strands up top.

"Celia?" Murph had turned back to me with an expectant stare.

I glanced over his shoulder to even more staring eyes that looked away when he shot them another glare.

"So you wanna go with me? I know it's last minute but …"

I gave him a small smile and watched in horror as his smile faded. Saying no to him sucked.

"It's cool," he said with a nod, already knowing my answer.

But I still needed to explain. "I'm sorry, Murph. I'm not feeling us. I wish I were, I do. But I will be there, probably hanging with Mer and Jacob. I'd like to dance, as long as your much more deserving date is all right with that."

He nodded again with pressed lips. "I get it. And I would like that too." His eyes flitted around. "I should, uh ..."

"Yeah. See ya," I said, watching him walk off with the others before shooting my gaze back to Caleb. He was chatting with two girls who had wandered over to him and his friend.

"Celia!" Mer's scream traveled down to me and everyone else within a mile radius.

Caleb's face lifted toward the Ferris wheel then instantly dropped to the ground, searching. His eyes skipped past me then backtracked and locked on. The stare was intense, cutting through me with something like lightning, connecting us for so long. His eyebrows furrowed.

"Celia hurry!" Mer called down to me again. "Take this picture!"

Caleb broke contact first, glancing up at Mer then over at the girl talking beside him.

I finally spun around and looked up. Mer waved from their bucket, which had stopped at the top as others got on below. She and Jacob were standing upright and started to kiss. I fumbled my camera and took the shot as security guards brushed past me on their way to the wheel. Crap.

Mer screamed excitedly again, and the wheel started to move. I glanced back over at Caleb, feeling a pull to go to him. Only, knowing Mer could be in trouble, I went to her instead. They were also met by the two security guards, who cut their wristbands and booted them from the fair, but not before Mer ran, dancing and singing and tiring the guards out. Jacob and I had to corral her and convince her to leave before the cops were called.

"Aw, man. I don't want to ruin your night. I'm sorry." Mer hugged me close and shot a finger over her shoulder to the guards as we passed the main ticket booths.

"What about my night?" Jacob asked.

"Hey, you are an accomplice, buddy. I wasn't the only one up there," she joked. "Besides, my parents aren't home right now, so …"

Jacob shut his mouth right up with a Cheshire cat worthy smile.

I laughed then pried Mer off me. "I'm staying."

"Yeah?" she asked, the lights of the fair reflecting inside her excited light brown eyes. "Yay! Good. I can come back and pick you up—"

"I saw Caleb inside." I hitched a thumb over my shoulder and tried my best to keep my expression neutral even though my body was trembling with anticipation. "I'm sure he'll take me home."

"I'm sure he will," Jacob murmured.

Mer tilted her head at him and narrowed her eyes. When she looked back at me, she asked seriously, "Yeah? You sure?"

"Yeah. Or I'll call my mom if not. No problem. Have a good rest of your night."

"Text me." She kissed her palm then blew that kiss to me before turning and running through the parking lot.

When I got back into the fairgrounds, Caleb was no longer in line at the haunted house. So I waited at the side by some smelly trash cans, hoping what I was about to do wouldn't wreck our friendship. It had already suffered enough. I didn't want to lose him completely. I'd known for a while how much he'd meant, though, how much I felt about him. I'd let so many things cloud my head, deter me from seeing what was so plain to see. He was completely right for me. Daring. Funny. Sexy. Frustrating. Pushy. Smug. Thoughtful.

Way more than fine.

Holding my breath—because of the trash smell, not nerves—I caught sight of him as he jumped out of a seat behind his friend. His eyes traveled around the crowd as if he were looking for someone. He moved forward, and I did the same, feeling like a creepy stalker. But I needed the right moment. I didn't want to screw it up.

Payback was what I was after.

He got a soda from a concession booth then moved toward the darkened stage area set up for bands to perform. While his friend headed for a row of porta-potties, he leaned against a rail fence and kicked a foot onto the base to wait. *Perfect.*

I snuck around the backside of the concession booth and came up from behind him as he watched the crowd pass by.

"RAHH!" I lunged forward into sight.

"AHHH!" His soda launched into the air as his body scrambled backward.

I couldn't stop the cackling laugh that escaped me. I'd done it. "Ha! Oh my God. I got you. I so got you."

"Dammit," Caleb replied, dropping his hand from the imaginary set of pearls he'd been clutching before standing up straighter and looking around to check if anyone had witnessed the epic scare.

People had seen, and they were amused. Especially his friend, who had returned from the bathroom and was now laughing at him with me.

"Nice one," the friend said. I recognized his face from school but didn't know him. "Hi."

"Celia, Devon," Caleb introduced us with a swipe of his hand through the air.

"Hi," I replied with a smile then refocused on Caleb, my smile only growing more.

Devon cleared his throat. "Yo, man. I just remembered who that girl was at the funnel cake stand. Hit me up later."

"Later." Caleb tracked Devon's movements until he disappeared into the crowd. His eyes shifted around some more. "Where's Mer?"

"She got booted."

"Oh. You didn't bail with them?" His eyes dropped to the ground, looking at my feet as I kicked the railing's post with the toe of my Chucks, my nerves finally taking over.

"No. I was kinda hoping you could give me a ride home when you leave. Or I can call my mom if you can't. No big. I just wanted to get some more pics for my portfolio." I held my camera out from around my neck as if that was going to help prove something.

"Yeah. Okay." He nodded.

"I mean, if you're busy or meeting someone else ..."

"Nope. Lead the way," he said, his eyes watching me carefully.

He wasn't joking or playing around like normal, only acting reserved, which made me a bit uneasy. Maybe I'd made a mistake. Maybe I was asking too much. Maybe he'd changed his mind while mine finally stopped denying the truth.

I took a few uninspired shots, fully aware of where he was at all times—close to my side or watching from behind. My mind wouldn't let me focus. He hadn't said anything more to me, and it was driving me insane.

Standing, I turned away from the Ferris wheel to him.

"Okay. That's plenty. I'm sorry if I wasted your time." His silence was crushing me. "I can wait by the front ticket booth. If you wanna stay, you can text me when you're ready. Or maybe I should call my mom."

"If that's what you want," he said simply, digging his hands into his jean pockets.

No, it wasn't what I'd wanted. I wanted to feel him against me. I wanted to kiss those smart-ass lips.

I tucked my camera into my shoulder bag and took a few steps closer. His eyes closed with a long blink, and his chest expanded with a deep breath.

"I have to tell you something," I admitted as his face tipped downward. "I wasn't sure, and I was also afraid of things changing …"

"Yeah?"

"I …"

"Celia …"

"I … have an answer." I bit my lip and stared up into his eyes as I recalled what he'd asked at the abandoned house last fall. "You and me? It wouldn't be so bad."

He released a long breath, and I couldn't tell exactly what it meant. His eyes closed again. His face remained stoic. He'd said I'd had to decide for myself. He wouldn't push. I needed to.

With shaky hands, I pressed one against his chest and lifted the other to the side of his neck, drawing his attention and his face down as I stepped closer. "I can't stop thinking about you. I miss you. I want more with you."

He sighed then a smile appeared, little at first and then full-blown with teeth. "It's about fucking time, Tarsier."

I giggled at that and his arms were instantly around me, wrapping down at my waist, fingertips digging in.

"We won't be so bad," he whispered then brushed his lips to mine, softly, sweetly.

I lifted my other hand to his face, grabbing hold, pulling him in more. And then we were kissing, mouths opening, needing a deeper connection. His tongue licked inside, and I let him, tasting him with my own. He made a sound like a hum and his fingers dug deeper into my lower back, eliminating any remaining space between us, crushing me against his hard body. He felt divine. Strong yet soft. Every touch of his hands, every motion of his mouth, both firm and gentle.

My body weakened, overloaded with feeling as it released the tension I'd felt moments before. He hadn't changed his mind. I couldn't believe I'd been so blind because everything clicked in a single moment.

He broke contact, lifting his face to the night sky with a deep breath.

"Are you okay? Was that …?" The kiss felt perfect to me. More than. Maybe he didn't feel the same.

His face tipped back down to me with another gorgeous smile on his lips. "I am well past okay. And that was so incredible. Better than I ever imagined. And damn, I have imagined it a lot." Those lips pushed against mine again.

I giggled. "I, uh, I owe you a soda."

"You owe me nothing. I'd sacrifice a thousand more sodas if this is the outcome."

"No need for sacrifices."

"No?" His head turned back and forth. "How about an obligatory fair game stuffed animal then? Or maybe even some time in the photo booth over there? I get it now. I totally understand all the girly, mushy shit. Suddenly, I'm wanting to do it all right now. For you."

I couldn't stop the smile on my face even if I wanted to. "Are you getting cheesy on me?"

"Tell me what you want. I will do it all. I'm not even the least embarrassed to admit that shit."

"I want you."

"You have me."

19
Celia

-now-

"**A**nd they didn't say anything about sleeping out here?" I asked Caleb, looking over my shoulder at the blankets and pillows he'd gotten from the lodge.

"Lucy, the receptionist, mentioned that this parking area and the quarry itself are still state land. So while they help maintain the space, they technically aren't responsible for it and won't do anything as long as we aren't a pain in the ass. She may have already called me one, though."

I laughed at that. "Yeah, I'm sure. What did you have to do to get all this?"

"Nothing much. Promise my first born male feline's paw in cat marriage."

As I laughed again, I shivered. My bikini was still damp, my hair too.

"It's getting cold," he noted, rubbing my bare thighs, still standing between them.

I scooted farther out on the edge of the tailgate and reached up, drawing his face to mine, kissing him softly, thoroughly enjoying the way his scruff tickled and scratched at my skin, and the way he let me control the tempo, the rhythm.

His hands slid higher up my thighs and gave a firm squeeze before breaking our lips apart. "You should get dry before we film the intro for the task. Lucy also mentioned us being able to use their outdoor bathroom attached to the lodge, which she says is nicer than the bathrooms out here. No one's around, though. So you could change in the back seat if you want."

I nodded, and he helped me hop down. After an awkward minute swapping my clothes in the cab, I reemerged in my shorts, flats, and T-shirt to find him already changed into a pair of cargo shorts, a thin gray V-neck, and the pair of slip-on sandals he'd worn earlier.

"You need to stop ogling my sexy body before I start to feel objectified."

"Smug as ever," I replied with an eye roll.

He laughed, grabbed my hand, then yanked me to his body, practically folding himself entirely around me. His warmth felt spectacular, but so did his grasp. Flexed arms wrapping tightly, fingers clutching, face resting on the top of my head—he held me like he never wanted to let go, and it was the best feeling in the world. So good I sighed.

"Let's do this." He stepped away, grabbed the notebook, and made some annotations in the extra pages after the list. Those held the dates and places of the tasks we'd completed, with empty space for all the others. "I find it hard to believe you never slept under the stars. She did that summer."

I pointed to the date. "I went to visit my grandparents with my mom then, right after graduation." Unlike the previous summer, I'd been so grateful to get away.

"Right. That wasn't long before I went to football camp."

I looked down sadly at the notebook. "I was happy I didn't have to see you."

His fingers slipped under my chin and lifted my face. "I was relieved that I didn't have to see you either. It wasn't that I didn't want to. Because I wanted to, like I wanted nothing else. It was that I knew I would cave on my promise to Mer if I was around you at all. I couldn't be near you and not be with you. It hurt so fucking bad. Knowing that I'd hurt you made it a hundred times worse. Now I only wish I could erase it all."

"I'm angry with her. I don't want to be, but I am."

"I am too. That's why it took me a few days to process what she was asking. I should have done many things differently, including what happened at the wake. But I'm not sure what I would have done if she hadn't asked this of us." His hand slid over my jaw, cradling my face.

"I wouldn't have answered your calls or your texts, I know that. I was so angry. So after everything, I'm glad she did this, and I'm especially happy that you chose to show up at my apartment."

"I'm happy you didn't shoot me when I did."

"Not a chance," I admitted with a smile. "If anything, I would have stabbed you. I was too hungover for gunshots."

"Ohhh!" he said, throwing his head back with a laugh. His gaze was one of adoration when his face tipped back down. He pressed his lips to my forehead for a few moments. "We better get to this. We're losing the light."

I readied the GoPro and started recording while he grabbed hold of the urn. We moved to a group of trees off to the side of the parking area.

"So we're staying the night here at the quarry to do two more tasks Celia didn't complete senior year. Sleep under the stars and watch a sunrise. The bed of my truck is home for the next few hours."

I panned the camera around to get a shot of the truck and the pillows and blankets inside.

"Hopefully, this doesn't end up being something like *The Blair Witch Project*—"

I gasped behind the camera.

"Oh shit. Sorry, Celia." He chuckled.

"You are not sorry," I said, still focused on him as darkness continued to overtake the sky, the water and cliff already like the deep shadows in a dusk painting. There was no moon. Everything would disappear soon enough.

"Maybe not." He shrugged, and I reached forward and slugged his arm. "Ow. Okay. We are perfectly safe here, people. There's a cabin close. I'm sure it has plenty of places to hide and maybe trip and fall. Also likely lots of sharp blades hanging from hooks in the basement."

"Caleb!" I screeched and looked around.

"I'm just saying. And you know, couples always seem to get hit first—"

"Okay, I can't do this. Take me home."

"No, no, no," he said in a rush as he darted forward and grabbed hold of me, tossing my arms up around his neck. "I will hold you all night if you need me to." His face nuzzled against my neck, scruff scratching my skin, lips pressing beneath my ear.

My body flashed with heat, and I lifted my eyes to the sky, watching the stars begin to show. "Oh, you are so smooth, aren't you? Don't worry, I'll get you back."

"I have no doubt you will," he whispered with a breathy laugh then backed away and opened the urn. "Where was I? Oh, yeah ... So if you're seeing this, please tell our families—"

"Caleb!"

He laughed with his mouth wide and stuck out his tongue. Mother eff … My body caught fire. Even with the light almost totally gone, his full smile threatened to melt my heart and my underwear.

"Sorry. Okay. So, here's to Mer. I'm sure she would have approved of our choice to stay because she would have thought of it first." He unscrewed the urn lid and shook some ashes at the base of a tree. "Anything to add, Tarsier?"

I groaned at the nickname, mostly because he used it directly on camera, which I wasn't sure had happened yet. Either way, many more people would hear it. Know it.

"Oh, crap." He shuffled over to me. "That slipped. Honest. We'll edit it." As I let the camera fall to my side, he brushed some hair back from my face. "Are you tired? Hungry?"

"Actually, I am a little hungry. Do you have any more of those fantastic pb&j's stashed somewhere?"

"Nope. But they have to have food up there," he said. "Give me a minute." And he was off into the dark, leaving me all alone.

I scurried back to the bed of the truck and lay flat inside to stare up at the stars, now brighter than anything else, but also because I feared some knife-wielding lunatic would get out of the water and slice me open. Maybe not exactly that, but I wasn't hung up on the specifics.

Caleb returned in the nick of time, before I started sinking into true paranoia and analyzing every leaf rustle, owl hoot, and twig snap.

"You don't want to know what I had to do for these. Here, hop out and hold them, and I'll spread the blankets."

I slipped off the tailgate and took the paper plate he offered. The smell hit me before I even focused on what it was.

Sweet. Warm sugar and chocolate. Cookies. "Oh, these smell like heaven. Tell me you got milk."

"Of course." His body shifted around, covering the bed. "The comforter will soften the bottom a little better. But if the thinner blankets aren't warm enough tonight or we aren't comfortable, we can sleep in the cab the rest of the time. I'm sure that'll still count. Hop up." He set his sandals at the edge, dug into his pockets, and pulled out two milk bottles. I handed the cookies over, climbed up, and kicked off my flats.

"Mmm." The cookies tasted as good as they smelled.

"Right?" He chewed one down quickly. "So did ya miss me?"

"I did, especially after that delightful commentary on our potential deaths by a scary woodland witch or the dude with the mask who likes to kill people at Camp Crystal Lake."

He chuckled. "Why didn't you use your phone flashlight?"

"I checked it earlier when I got dressed and it's almost dead. I might fight you for your charger when we leave in the morning."

"No need to fight. I'll give you anything."

"Anything, huh?" I mumbled, chewing the last of the cookie down then chasing it with my milk.

"That's what I said, Tarsier." He bit into another.

"Hmm. That's pretty risky. I could ask you for, well, anything. Are you sure you don't want to reconsider?"

"Nah. I trust you." After downing his milk, he lay back, tucked a pillow under his head, and stretched out with a satisfied sigh.

I followed his lead, grabbing the GoPro and tilting it up to the clear, inky sky dotted enchantingly by the stars. A perfect night.

"So what's it gonna be?" he whispered.

"I'll get back to you," I replied, not sure what I'd use that kind of power on yet. "This is incredible. I'm glad you asked me to stay. Thank you." I turned the camera and my face to the side to see him, finding his eyes already on me. Only a dim glow lit his features, but his eyes seemed to shine.

"Thank you for staying." His hand found my free one and brought it to his lips to kiss my knuckles sweetly. "Tell me something."

"What?" I asked, turning my attention back to the stars as he kept hold of my hand.

"Anything. Tell me more. You know, to really drive home what I've been missing these years."

I chuckled. "I don't know. I'm kinda the same. I have my usual routine. Workouts are essential because I love to eat everything. My job pays the bills. My apartment's nice—"

"With a guard neighbor who sized me up before I could enter the building."

That one made me laugh fully. "Mrs. Thomas. Oh yeah, she had a few things to say about that morning." She'd been very eager to grill me when I'd returned home that night.

"I bet. She was excited to witness a *Maury* level event in person, I'm sure." After a pause, he asked, "What else?"

"I have four close friends from work. We go out for drinks whenever their schedules mesh. They're all older. Some married. Some with kids. You might have to thank them one day, for me being more compliant when you showed up at my apartment."

"Yeah?"

"We were out last Friday. We talked about the wake and about you. They may have softened me up on the idea of speaking to you again, to at least let you apologize correctly."

"Well, I will have to thank them then. What else? What's your favorite flower?"

I bit my lip and squeezed his hand. "You know that one."

"Do I? Wasn't it a lily or something?" I could hear the smile in his voice.

"Once upon a time, back before the most annoying boy I knew gave me a daisy." His thumb stroked my hand at that. "What about you?"

"Me? It's a toss-up. Venus flytraps and daisies."

"Stop," I joked, shaking my head.

"No, seriously. The flower on the flytrap is nice, and the plant is a badass."

"And the daisy?" I humored him.

"Well, it's elegant, and though it may look simplistic, it has a lot more going on because it's actually many flowers. The outside petals—soft and gorgeous—are individual florets. Then there's the center cluster, with more of a different floret, which is so attractive to any pushy, nectar craving bee. And bright yellow too, like a certain bikini I remember."

If it had been daytime, he would have seen how red my face had gotten. But I doubted he needed to see to know.

"You seem to know a lot about daisies." I whispered with a smile. "And?"

"Hmm. Football is still close to my heart. *Here we go, Steelers!* I have a few close friends from work and college. We hang here and there. I go to the gym to maintain this notch-above-average bod you were appreciating earlier." I laughed as he continued, "I do like long walks on the beach whenever I visit one. I'm not big on social media."

"I remember."

"Yeah? You stalkin' me?"

"Well, we're still friends on Facebook, though I don't think I've seen you post anything since high school," I admitted. "Not that I'm on there much either. What else?"

"Hmm. I'm preparing a proposal for my dad to expand, like with the custom designs I've done on the side for some great clients. I made several interactive kids sets for local pediatric clinics. It was really fun to see them in use." His hand squeezed mine again, and my heart felt as if it were going to overflow. "What do you think? Did I share the right things? Are you convinced of my awesomeness?"

"If I didn't know you better, I'd say you were so full of it. But after hearing your awesomeness, I'm feeling disappointed in myself. You are fascinating, talented, and endearingly smug like always. While I …"

His body shifted, turning over onto his side, propping his head onto his hand. "Don't even think about it. I saw you today with your camera. Damn, Celia. I know you love it. And you're not just good. You've always been amazing. Those pictures in your apartment … They are incredible."

"Yeah, but it's one of those things that seems unobtainable."

"Why?"

"I could try to find a job around where I am that will hire, sure. But entry or assistant positions aren't the best pay. And if I wanted to start my own company … Well, my current student debt situation severely limits start-up costs. It'll be a while before anything like that could happen."

"I see your points. But have you tried? Have you done the numbers or maybe inquired at a bank to get a loan?"

"No. I didn't want the heartbreak of denial, or being crushed when a side gig crashes and burns."

"You owe yourself the chance. You need to give it a shot or you'll be stuck where you are forever."

"I never minded, I guess. Maybe that's the sad part."

"That's understandable too. I thought I was happy, until Mer died, and until you walked into her room. Most other shit feels meaningless. I've wasted so much time, like all the times I didn't take off work when she was home to visit, believing that there would be another trip soon enough. And after seeing you again, all that time without you felt the same. I can't go back. And I don't want you to settle for less, even if it means a crash might come after that fall."

"I've missed you. For so many reasons. Before I stepped into Mer's room, I felt like I was sleepwalking. Going along. Not really knowing, not really feeling. Seeing you again ... you woke me up. I haven't felt this good in so long." I dropped the GoPro to my chest and switched it off, realizing I'd been filming the entire time, not focusing on the stars and the night at all.

"Come here," he said, shifting closer, lifting his hand to my cheek.

His palm was warm, his lips even more so as they parted mine. The kiss was slow at first, lazy and seductive, promising, building. His body leaned in more, pushing me fully onto my back, taking over, driving his tongue inside. My whole body heated and shivered at the same time, my nerves alerted to every touch, every connection, firing off sparks of excitement. His fingers dipped into my hair as he turned his head and mine, mouth moving, ebbing and flowing in a sensual rhythm.

I pressed my hands to his waist and slipped them under his shirt, needing to touch his skin. As soon as I made contact, a fuse between us ignited. His mouth became the force to tip my whole world, demanding and urgent. I squeezed his hips, yanking him down, desperate to feel him everywhere.

A low moan rumbled in his throat, making me yearn for even more.

His mouth broke away from mine, trailing kisses over my chin, my jaw, my neck.

"Caleb," I whispered.

"Celia." He spoke my name onto my skin like a prayer. "I don't want to stop this, but I will if you don't want—"

"Don't stop. Please don't stop." I dropped my hands to the hem of my own shirt and wiggled beneath him.

He took my cue, nearly ripping his shirt off while I did the same. And then he was back down on me, palm pressing to my stomach and sliding upward as his mouth met mine again. His hand cupped a breast, massaging over my too-padded bra.

"Front clasp," I murmured in a break of the kiss and trailed my hands between us, up his abs to his toned chest.

He got the message, freeing the clasp with a quick movement. "Fuck. You are so much more than I remember, everything I ever wanted."

My nipples were rock-hard as his fingers pinched at one. I sighed into his mouth and arched my back, pushing myself into his hand more.

And then his mouth was on the move again. Down. Down. Licking my skin, kissing the tender flesh of my breast, and hitting home with the other nipple. His mouth took it in, tongue swirling slowly before sucking.

With my fingers in his hair, I tried my best to maintain some level of control when all I wanted was to jump on top of him as soon as possible. I didn't care about where we were, about who might catch a glimpse through the blackened night. I was only thinking of him and how I'd wanted this to happen so long ago. With the darkness, I was tempted to believe it was a dream, and I'd wake up in my apartment alone and sad. But I knew it wasn't true. His touch was hot and firm, the air cool and calm, and Caleb and I were finally going to have sex.

20

Caleb

-now-

She made little sounds. Whimpers. Like fucking music to my ears. Damn, how did this happen? My brain was short-circuiting, wanting to speed up and slow down at the same time, urging me to take my mouth south, taste even more of her, while my dick was harder than Intermediate Accounting and wanted nothing more than to purge all the numbers.

I was stuck on her flawless breasts, giving them every bit of the focus I could manage while attempting to decide. I supposed it was punishment for not being prepared for this scenario. There had been no plan to stay overnight. I expected to be home already, imagining this very scene under the hot water of my shower, stroking myself while picturing these perfect breasts and her soft skin.

Fuck me. I was on the verge of nutting in my shorts just thinking about the reality of it.

She moaned and tugged at my hair, and my decision was made. There would be other times. For now, here out in the open, under the night sky for all the animals and maybe even a curious lurker within range to see, we were getting down to business.

I slid my hand to her shorts, unbuttoning. She took over quickly, undoing her own so I could get mine. We both shimmied for a few moments, kicking off the rest of our clothes. I moved back to her sweet lips, savoring the residual deliciousness of chocolate chip cookie lingering there. Her legs parted as my hand slid up her thigh, stopping only when I felt her warmth, trying to see without seeing, enjoying the feel of her trimmed hair. I wanted my face there. To breathe her in and taste her.

She moaned when I slid my finger over her, and I echoed the same reaction when I suddenly felt her hand wrap around my dick.

And that was when I remembered again that I hadn't been fully prepared. "Shit," I said, both as a statement of pleasure and anger at myself. "Celia, shit. Shit." Her hand stroked down me once, twice …

"Shit," I said again and broke away from her. "I need a condom." After glancing around, I vaulted over the side of the truck buck naked with a hard-on that had the power to cut through all the limestone inside the quarry. Her cute giggle followed behind me.

Please. Please. Please.

I dug into the glove box, then the front and back console, then looked under the seats. It had been a long time since I'd had a stash in my truck. There was always the pull-out option, but I'd much rather—

"There's one in my bag," Celia said, making me stand upright and look around the doorframe. In the near blackness, I could barely see her face, but it seemed like her head was tilted.

"Thank God," I said, lunging for her bag and rooting inside

while more giggles met my ears. She was ready, and man, that made me feel even better.

I was back into the bed within ten seconds, kneeling at her feet.

Seeing her sprawled in the bed of my truck, shadowed in the night with only a faint glow from the stars and the distant lights of the lodge, had me choked up. "Wow."

"What?" she whispered but made no move to cover herself. She was relaxed and comfortable, with me, with this.

"It's just that I …" I had no words. As much as I wanted to express, I was speechless.

"Caleb …"

I ripped the wrapper, rolled that sucker on, and crawled between her legs, kissing her smooth stomach, taking soft nips of her flesh along the way up. She spread her legs wider as I settled in between them. Her hands splayed over my back, gripping, encouraging. After a long, deep kiss, I looked into those big eyes, angled my hips, then flexed forward, entering her as slowly as I could manage as she accepted me.

Her fingernails dug into my back and the most incredible sigh escaped her lips, expressing exactly what we both felt, the years slipping away, finally bringing us together. And it was so much more than I'd ever thought it could be.

"I want so much with you." I kissed her neck then retreated from her for only a moment before pushing back inside in another long stroke.

"Yes. You …" She arched her back and rotated her hips, making me moan. "That's the anything I want you to give me. Give me you."

"You've always had me." Another flex, another sigh. "You were always with me." I kissed her lips then pushed myself up to stare into her eyes again. They watched me adoringly as I slammed my hips to her, harder this time. "Anytime I saw silky brown hair with a face hidden by a camera. Every time I saw a daisy." My pace quickened, greedy with need, wanting to feel so much.

The comforter moved under us, sliding with every thrust, shifting us closer to the cab.

She squeaked a tiny laugh, lifted her arms, and braced her palms against the truck to keep her head from hitting.

I curled my back and dipped my face to her breasts, licking and sucking on a nipple. My muscles came alive, energized for her. I moaned onto her skin, and my hips worked harder.

"Oh, yes," she murmured. "I ... this ..."

"You feel incredible," I replied, cherishing her, never wanting the connection to end. "You are everything."

Her breaths came faster, shorter with every thrust, and her whimpers grew louder, blending together into the sweetest and most erotic sound.

"Caleb. Caleb. Ah. I'm ..."

She unraveled beneath and around me, her body clenching tight, sending me over the edge with her.

"Celia." Her name was a strained breath as an orgasm took hold. "Fuck." I dipped down slowly even though I wanted to collapse. But I didn't want to hurt her. The truck was hard as hell. There was no way I'd crush her into it.

Her hands moved from their braced positions to my cheeks, stroking as I leaned down more for a kiss.

"Oh, ooh," I mumbled as she shifted beneath me. She chuckled against my lips. So fucking sweet. "Are you all right?"

"More than," she replied, sliding her hands down my neck and onto my shoulders.

"This wasn't exactly comfortable. I promise I will make it up to you. Thoroughly." I kissed her chastely before moving my lips to her neck. "I have plans that don't include having to worry about peeping animals. So many plans. I need to taste all of you. My delicious daisy."

"Does that make you the pushy bee?"

"Oh yeah. A thirsty carpenter bee," I whispered then licked up her neck.

She shivered. Whether it was from the feeling or more from the warmth of sex dwindling away, the cool air registering once again, I backed away from her and grabbed the two thinner blankets, spreading them over her body before tying off the condom and jumping out of the truck to toss it in the trash.

When I crawled back onto the tailgate, she was sitting upright watching. "Are you still up for sleeping out here or do you want to get into the backseat?"

"No, this is good, but I need your heat."

"Yes, ma'am."

She held open the blankets for me, and I slid inside and settled onto my back. Her body wrapped around me, head against my chest, arm and leg draped over me. I nuzzled my nose into her hair, inhaled, then released a contented sigh. Perfect. There was nothing better.

"Should we get dressed?" she asked, her voice sleepy, exhaustion setting in from the excitement of the day.

I yawned, feeling the hit too. "No fucking way."

Her body shook against mine with a silent laugh. After a moment, she said, "I'm a little upset that you weren't my first. I wish this had happened then."

"Me too," I agreed somberly. But instead of dwelling, I focused on the ridiculously accurate truth and added, "I would have given you the best four minutes of your life." She laughed audibly this time. "And three of those would have been like watching a hilarious silent, Charlie Chapman style film titled The Boy and the Condom."

Her body vibrated more, shaking the entire truck. After a huge gasping breath, she said, "Oh my God, stop!"

"Exactly what you would have said then."

"You are such a liar. You had already done it. You had experience."

"So? Even if I had done it a thousand times, it would have been you. You, who could bring me to my knees with one look of your glorious eyes, one touch of your soft hands, one whisper from your lips. I would have died that night. I would have been so fucking happy, but I would have died inside you. I only lived tonight because I've been dreaming about it for so much longer."

Her head shifted back so she could look at me. "You had me spinning, Caleb Samuels. You had me cussing a lot, and screaming with fright, but also spinning."

I squeezed her in closer, drawing her face up and dipping mine to the side to meet her lips. "I would love to go for round two right now, but I think we should sleep since we have to see the sun rise and get you to work. Also, I'd probably break off my kneecaps."

"Not if I'm on top."

"Oh, Tarsier. Don't tempt me or you'll be missing work with me tomorrow … and maybe even all week."

21
Caleb

-now-

"Celia. Time to wake up," I whispered into her ear, keeping her tucked inside my curl. Being her big spoon was the greatest. There was no hiding my morning wood pressed against her ass. I inhaled her hair again and squeezed my arm tighter, palming her breast.

That got a lovely moan in response. "It's still dark."

"Sunrise, we gotta see it. It's on the list."

"Did it specify in there that we had to stay up to watch the sunrise? I can't remember." She coughed a little to clear away the sleepy rasp in her voice.

"It doesn't say. But we could do that another time on our own."

"That sounds good." With a slow turn, she lay on her back, her eyes blinking to focus on mine.

"Morning, beautiful."

"Now I know you are a liar. I wake up with myself every day and there's no way that—"

"It was always my favorite time to see you," I cut off her

words with my truth. "Whenever you stayed the night, I lived to see you in the morning. Sleepy eyes. Sleepy body."

"You teased me every morning I was there. You'd swat my hair and call me feral."

"Yeah, I did. I wanted so badly to have your hair in my face like this morning."

"You should have told me something instead of teasing me."

"I should have done a lot of things, but there's no time to think about it." I reached for the GoPro and started filming. "Good morning." I held the camera out and pointed it toward me, then her, then both of us.

She swatted my hand away.

"Don't mind her," I said to the camera lens with a laugh. "We have no coffee. But good news!" I reached for the notebook and opened the list. "We're knocking out this sunrise task right now. I need to find Mer first, so hang on a second." After setting the camera down, pulling on my clothes, and shoving the notebook into my back pocket, I went into the cab for the urn then jumped back into the bed.

Celia clasped her bra and pulled her T-shirt on. She looked at me with an eyebrow raised.

"So damn sexy," I murmured, receiving a smile in return. "Should we climb for it?"

"That would be great. I can get some shots." In another minute, her shorts were on and her camera hung from her neck.

We both made a quick bathroom trip then I handed over the GoPro, and she started filming again as I shook ashes into a tissue. "She'll stay up top this time."

We crested Eagle's Nest with about a minute to spare, the dark sky fading with each passing second. I took hold of the GoPro again and watched as Celia snapped off many shots with a look of concentration in her pressed lips and scrunched eyebrows.

Turning the camera to eye the lens with the horizon behind me, I said, "This is it. Check out this gorgeous view." I panned around, pointing at Celia first. She caught me and gave me a side-eye glare before getting back to her shots. I laughed and continued on to the pink and orange hues of the wispy clouds as the sun made its appearance. Squatting down near one of the bushes along the backside of the cliff, I shook the ashes into the soft soil and filmed it. A few moments later, I found myself back over at the edge, focusing on the lodge and its dark windows. Nothing was moving, and nothing probably would for quite a while.

"Celia."

"Yeah?" She lay down at the edge to capture a few downward shots of the cliff and the still water, a mirror image fifty feet below.

"There's another task we need to do. Right now."

"What? Caleb, we need to go."

"Stay, please. Go in late. Say you had an appointment or that you had an asshole accost you."

"I don't think that's a good idea. We really should get back down."

I conceded only to come up with an idea of how to convince her on the way down. It was a risky one.

When we returned to the parking area, she started to cross over the rocky ground to the Silverado. But my feet took me to the sandy strip by the water.

"Okay, everyone. We're doing another one."

"Caleb!" Celia whisper-yelled at me from the truck, her face darting one way then the other, afraid she'd wake someone.

I whipped out the notebook and pointed the lens at the page. "I'll scatter more ashes for this after. Right now, we're daylight skinny-dipping."

"Caleb!" Celia said, the horror still very much heard inside the next whisper-yell. "What are you doing?"

With a laugh, I stuffed the book back into my pocket, angled the camera down, then wrenched off my shirt and dropped it close to the edge.

Her eyes bugged out as soon as my shorts dropped next. "We can't ... we shouldn't do this right now."

"No one's awake. What better time? I'm pushing you, Celia. Right now. Live with me in this moment."

She hesitated for only a second then surprised the fuck out of me by setting her camera into the truck and stalking toward me.

I slipped into the frigid water carefully, keeping my eyes and the GoPro aimed at her.

"Drop the camera," she said, lifting the hem of her shirt and pausing until I obeyed her command. Her top and bra were off the next moment, igniting my cold body with a fire kindled not only of desire but also pride and wonder. She was more daring and braver than ever.

I sucked in a breath when she kicked off her shorts and underwear. And only then did she look around before slipping in with me. Angling the lens to my face, I made sure her body was submerged then included her in the shot, still keeping it at neck level in case the sun was already powerful enough to cut beneath the surface of the crystal water.

"So another task down. We'll have to see what's next, but for now, here ya go, Mer." I rushed through that shit as fast as I deemed respectful and set the camera on top of our clothes.

Maybe it was a little too quick. But I doubted many people would care, knowing that I was currently looking at the most stunning creature in the world all wet under the rising sun. Yeah, no one would care. Not even Mer.

"Oh, baby. Maybe I did die after all," I whispered, drifting farther out.

She smiled shyly. "You sure know how to make me feel good."

"Come here. I want to make you feel better." I took her hand and yanked her closer, wrapping an arm around her slick skin and anchoring her to me. I kissed her hard, slipping my thigh between her legs and gripping her ass while we continued to tread to stay afloat. No ledges in a deep-ass quarry made it rough to do what I wanted to do. I reconsidered our position after a few minutes, thinking about moving back to the edge again, pin her to the rocks before we had to leave.

A scuffling sound caught my attention. I peeled my lips away from Celia and looked toward the water's edge. "Son of a ..."

"What?" Celia turned and gasped.

A boy, thin as a twig, no more than twelve, crouched over our things, snatching it all up into his arms.

"No, no, no, little boy," Celia pleaded. "Please don't do that."

His blond head lifted, and he stared right at us for a moment like a mouse caught stealing cheese. I was afraid to move, think-ing I'd spook him if I so much as breathed.

But then the little mother effer stood upright and darted off toward the clearing in front of the lodge. I scrambled into a swim, scooping and kicking the water harder than I'd ever had, no lon-ger caring about the noise. If it was only our clothes, I would have let him go. We had bathing suits in the truck we could have worn home. No problem. But he had the notebook—irreplaceable—and the GoPro, which had every second of footage from all the tasks on it because my dumb ass hadn't transferred any. The memory card was large. It didn't need any dumps.

"Fuck!"

I tracked his progress for as long as I could until I got to solid ground. The trees at the edge blocked my view enough for me to lose him. I headed in the same direction, hoping to spot him before he ducked indoors wherever he was staying, either the main lodge or the small cabins. Hustling past the trees, I glanced back once to see Celia still safely concealed inside the water, her head floating not too far from the edge. Good. Not that there was anyone around, but I didn't cherish the idea of her getting caught naked and alone.

Speaking of being seen ... I glanced up toward the vaulted windows on the backside of the lodge. Wide. Tall. And plenty of other little windows catching the morning's light and reflecting it back at me. I wouldn't even know if people were looking. The furniture on the back decks and room balconies were all empty.

I cupped my junk in one hand, calling it good enough as I jogged farther along.

One thing I hadn't thought about were the Adirondack chairs all positioned around a fire pit closer to the water. And that was a mistake. I realized that as soon as I ran past and heard giggling. Praying it was my imagination, I slowed and turned my head. Three women stared at me. Laptops in laps. Headphones on heads. Mouths wide-open.

I stopped moving, covering myself with both hands now, keeping my bare ass pointed toward the quarry water. Despite the strong urge to sprint away as fast as possible, I had no one to chase. The kid was gone.

"Ladies," I said with a tiny nod and a petrified smile. They blinked at me.

The one with the purple hair said, "Hey there ... naked guy." She turned to her friend with horn-rimmed glasses in the middle. "Where did he come from?"

"My dreams?" was her reply, drawing giggles from the other two.

"Uh ..." All right, things had gotten weird. "Did you happen to see the little kid who ran past here? He stole my stuff."

"Yeah, really skinny. Hey, you ever think of modeling? For book covers maybe?" Horn-rimmed asked.

Purple Hair smiled at her as if she had come up with the best idea ever.

What? "Uh, no. But I might think about it if you tell me what direction the kid ran." Hell, I was prepared to agree to just about anything to get out of that situation.

"He went around the lodge, toward the parking lot," the blonde on the end said, pointing over her shoulder while looking back down at her screen.

"Thanks." I took off while the other two jumped on her case.

"What? I'm on a deadline," was the last thing I heard.

When I rounded the side, the kid was jogging to a little trail that led to the cabins. His arms were empty. Panic set in, hitting me with a flash of heat that instantly made me sweat as I scanned the area, searching for a place he could have stashed our goods. A blue sedan idled toward the end of the lot, a heap of clothes lay beneath the driver's open window. I sprinted for it, and a guy with a bald buzz cut glanced at me before slamming on the gas and tossing more items from the window.

"You son of a bitch! Get back here!" I screamed and squinted at the dirty license plate, unable to read it. As soon as I got to the pile of clothes, I pulled on my shorts, grabbed the rest, then collected the trail of stuff on the way to the Silverado. My billfold. The GoPro. The notebook. It was all there. Even the cash and cards.

"What happened?" Celia asked when I returned to the water.

I held up one of the blankets and helped her out, shielding her in case more eyes were awake. "That blue sedan. Ford, I think. He must have paid the kid to grab our stuff. When I ran at the car, he took off and left it all behind."

She finished pulling on her shorts and slid into her top, forgoing the bra. "He left it all?"

"Yeah, nothing's missing." I dropped the blanket.

"That is odd. He has to be the one who filmed us before. I remember seeing that blue car."

"I remember it at Murph's place. It rode by a couple of times."

"Oh my God." She slapped her hands over her mouth. "He had to be in the parking lot all night if he followed us. Do you think he filmed at night?"

"If he did, he only got audio. Not that I'm thrilled about that either." I twisted my keys and walked to the truck with her. "As soon as we get back to my place, I'll contact Jay and Sam from the production team. Let them know."

"And I should probably call into work."

"You'll hear no argument from me," I said, thinking of all the things I'd like to do with her for the next several hours since I'd also be calling in.

She chuckled with a head shake. After packing up everything from the bed into the back seat, we hopped into the truck. I handed over my charger.

"You gonna tell me who you stopped to talk to over by the lodge?" she asked, biting her bottom lip as I pulled out of the parking area.

I sucked some air between my teeth. "So there were writers staying there. Well, a few were outside with their laptops."

A loud, quick fit of laughter burst from her. "I know this situation isn't funny. I was furious about that kid stealing our stuff. But I have to admit, watching you running naked ..." More broken giggles. "Your ass was glowing in the morning sunlight. That's something I will never forget. Going right into my laugh bank." She tapped a finger to her temple.

"I think you mean spank bank."

"Nope." She shook her head then slowly started to nod. "Okay, well, maybe it'll be filed there too."

22
Caleb

-then-

The urge to bust through Mer's door hit me like all the other times I'd done it. Then I heard Celia's happy voice somewhere on the other side, and I surprisingly refrained. My heart kicked into a heavy pace all the same, the cause no longer about the thrill but about her, anticipating the moment my eyes could take her in, my arms could wrap around her. It had been the same throughout the week, stolen moments at school or meeting after either or both of us had finished work.

Even though it had been an awesome week, those times still hadn't been nearly enough. I'd wanted so much more. Hours instead of moments. Entire days attached to those nighttime goodbyes. With summer approaching, the possibility of it happening was high, aside from my football camp and her upcoming visit to her grandparents. We'd have to spend as much time as we could before she left for State College in the fall. At least she would be close enough for weekend trips after that.

I tapped my knuckles on the door. "You guys decent?"

"Yeah," Mer answered.

With a breath, I pushed the door open, eager to see what was on the other side. Mer stood by her closet mirror in a blood red dress, curling the ends of her loose blond hair. Her eyes met mine in the reflection. "You look great, Mer." Unable to wait another second, I opened the door the rest of the way, scanning the opposite side of the room as I continued to speak. "Jacob might drop dead as soon as he sees—" Suddenly, all thought was gone.

Celia spun around in front of Mer's desk, and things went all slow motion for me. Her hair was pulled up in the back with wavy strands purposely escaping the hold. A few fell down at the edges of her face, which was decorated with a faint coating of makeup. Light green colored her lids, brightening the green rims of her big hazel eyes. Her top teeth bit her pink-stained pouty lower lip, holding down the shy smile pulling at the edges. Thin straps. Bare neck. Tops of her breasts peeking out above a straight, floor-length white dress with watercolor splatters of spring. Yellow. Pink. Green. Blue.

"Damn." I exhaled then swallowed thickly, my throat having dried up like a desert.

"She looks great, right?" Mer asked, rushing over to Celia before I could even take a step.

"Yeah, wow. Wow, Celia." I finally moved to her and stopped short, looking down at all the sawdust all over me. "I, uh …" Fuck. I wanted to wrap my arms around her and kiss her, but she was too perfect. I didn't want to mess her up. "You look so incredible."

"Thank you," she said as Mer released her and moved back to finishing her hair.

"I … have something for you. It's in my room. You have a sec?"

"Yeah," she said and followed behind me.

"The limo's here," Mer called after us. "Pictures out front in a minute!"

As soon as we stepped into my room, she said, "I'm so sorry that I couldn't get you a ticket this week. With the cutoff for the dinner seating and not finding any extras—"

"Stop apologizing for that. Besides, I would have had a helluva time finding a tux from the rental place in town at the last minute."

"Still," she said as I moved over to my desk. "I would rather you go, even if it meant wearing a baby blue suit from the seventies, ruffled shirt and all."

"Ha! I might have rocked it." I grabbed what I was looking for and turned to her.

Her eyes locked on the lifelike wooden daisy as I held it up by the stem and crossed the room. "I kinda messed up a couple petals with the chisel but was able to clean a good amount with the Dremel when I was sanding and detailing."

"You made this for me?" She pinched the stem to take hold.

"Yeah. You like it?"

"Do I like it? Psshhh." She ran a finger gingerly over the petals then cut her eyes to me. "It's so pretty. Thank you." Holding it out to the side, she leaned in close.

"No, I don't want to get you dirty—"

"Stop. I don't care if my dress gets sawdust on it. You better kiss me right now."

Okay then. I grabbed hold of her waist and pulled her body to mine while she lifted her arms onto my shoulders. She smelled so good. Flowery, fitting for her dress.

It still all felt unreal, and that was probably why I was so tentative at times, unsure of us, afraid to step over the line. From the moment we had our first kiss at the fair and all the others through the week, I kept thinking she was going to change her mind, decide I wasn't for her after all. But it wasn't the case right now. She was holding on to me tightly, fingers in my hair, palming the back of my head as I tasted her sweet lips, licked inside her delicious mouth. My mind thought of so many other things I wanted to do, all the places I wanted to kiss and lick along her body.

She pulled away enough to look into my eyes. "You're still meeting us at the fair, right?"

"I'll be there. I'm sorry we didn't do that Ferris wheel kiss last week. I didn't even think about it."

"We were both a little preoccupied," she admitted with a smile. "This is the last weekend to do it there, though. And Mer was right that it'll be fun to go after prom. I almost want to skip this and go do that with you."

"No, don't do that. You'll have a great time. It's prom. And maybe someone will spike the punch."

"I think that only happens in old movies," she said with a laugh, dipping her face against my chest.

"You're probably right. I'm sure someone will have drinks of the fun variety after."

"Well, I'll stay with Mer and Jacob since they are my ride to the fair, but after you get there and we do the Ferris wheel ... I don't want to stick around."

"No? I thought you said it would be fun?"

"I'd rather spend more time alone with you, maybe mark off another thing on my list."

Oh. That message went straight from my ears to my dick. Her big eyes looked up at me with a sexy stare, and I had to inhale deeply to calm myself. "I definitely, one hundred percent want that too. But I think my parents will be home. No privacy."

And The Beast was not an option. She deserved so much more than an old, cramped truck cab.

"My mom's out on her own date tonight. She won't be home."

"You have it all figured out, don't you?" I joked, trying to hide the fact that those words had obliterated my control. I was completely hard, and I was positive she felt it.

"I hope I do," she whispered before pulling my face down for another kiss.

"Yo!" Mer's voice cut through our connection, separating us. It wasn't like we'd hid what was happening from her, but we hadn't exactly been making out in front of her all week either. "Picture time."

"Great," Celia said, holding the wooden daisy close to her chest. "You coming down too?"

Mer answered, "Actually, I need to talk to Caleb a second."

"Oh! I'll meet you guys down there then," Celia said, tapping the daisy petals against her lips with a smile then walking out my door.

My eyes were still focused there when Mer rounded on me. Shaking her head, she said, "I thought I'd be fine with you two after this week, but you cannot do this to her."

"Do what to her? Date her? Pretty sure that's our business, not yours," I replied, irritation killing my good mood. I'd expected a little push back or warning flags from her about dating her best friend, but I hadn't expected a full-on stop sign slammed into my grill.

"You're right. Sure." She crossed her arms and stared at me pointedly. "But you seriously need to think about this, Caleb. She considered bailing out of prom tonight for you. Did she mention that?"

"Yeah, so what? We haven't had a bunch of time to spend together. She wanted to have more."

"Right. That's exactly it. I know where this is going. You've known her for a long time too, but you don't know her as well as I do. You will be her cage, Caleb."

"Cage? What the fuck are you talking about, Mer?" Anger replaced irritation in the span of a second.

"Come on, think about it. She's so reserved. You know this. If you get serious, there will be more skips down the road. Many more. Thank God State College is far enough away that she can't commute daily. She has to move out and stay in the dorms. With that comes experiences, you know? She deserves all of those. She needs to get out of here to live, to see more things, to do more things."

"She's going to do that. What are you freaking out about?"

"She won't if you're with her. You'll be here for your senior year. And if you're here, this is where she'll want to be, every weekend and any other chance she can get. She'll skip out on more things, more chances, more opportunities because she'll choose you over that. She'll choose the comfort of you, the time with you."

I felt as if she'd run me over.

"You know I'm right. I love her too much to see that happen. So don't do this to her, okay? I'm begging you."

"Shouldn't she be the one who makes this choice?" I asked, still wrecked by her words. I knew it was true. "Maybe I can talk to her about it. Maybe she won't need to come back here all the time."

"She will, and you know it. I won't be around. You'll be her closest friend and more if you decide to stay with her. She won't be interested in anything the campus has to offer because she will be wrapped up in you. If it's meant to work later, it will. But give her a chance to do something else. Give her that. She'll never get another shot at those experiences."

"I, uh …" I scrubbed my face with my hands, wanting to erase everything she said. But there was no chance at that. "We can have the summer. I don't think I can do this to her."

"And you think it'll be easier after you've spent more time together? It's been about a week." She drew in a deep breath and let it out with a long sigh. "I don't want her hurt either, but you need to realize that it's the best decision for her and for you. You have your own senior year to worry about too, your own shit to deal with. So, please … She needs that push now, Caleb. Like tonight after prom, now. You get too close and there's no going back."

"Mer! C'mon!" Celia's voice called up the stairs, giving me a jolt.

"I'll tell her you had to get a shower and that you'll see her later."

Not wanting to draw the conversation out any longer, I nodded then collapsed onto my bed as soon as she walked out.

I did shower after that, the task barely registering as I thought about what Mer had said. And even though I wanted to direct all my anger at her, to think of it all as bullshit, I knew she was right. And I couldn't justify being the one to hold Celia back when I wanted nothing more than for her to crack that shell herself and succeed.

The drive to the fair was also a blur as I debated how to handle it. In the end I knew there was no way I could stand in front of her and break her heart. For that, I was a coward, sure. Just not in the usual asshole way. It was because I had no chance of saying the words if I were to look into her eyes. I had wanted her for so long. To hold her. To taste her. To be around her as often as possible. To make her crazy as much as she'd made me insane by simply existing. I fucking loved her. It felt like I had for ages. So if I had to stand in front of her and look into those gorgeous eyes, my resolve would disappear.

The fair was a sea of dresses and tuxes. Jewelry sparkled under the twinkle of lights and so did the eyes of every couple I passed, my stomach twisting and knotting at the sight. That had been us the previous weekend. Holding hands. Kissing. My phone vibrated in my pocket. I spotted her near the Ferris wheel, standing beside Mer and Jacob, ready to get in line. She'd pulled her hair down entirely and was pressing the petals of the daisy I'd made her to her lips absently, as if she'd been holding it there all night. She probably had.

After tugging my phone out, I swiped the screen without checking the notification. It wouldn't have been anyone else.

Tarsier O.O: Where R U?

I watched her look around, her eyes searching. Using the side of the concession to hide, I texted back.

Me: I'm sorry. I can't come.

Tarsier O.O: What's wrong? Are you ok?

Me: Yeah. But I can't do this. We can't do this.

Tarsier O.O: Do what, Caleb? The fair?

Me: Us. It's not going to work. I thought it would, but I was wrong.

I looked up after I hit send and watched as she covered her mouth with the hand that held the daisy. I could almost hear her sob from fifty yards away and through all the moving bodies. Mer turned to her, catching her reaction. She put an arm around her. Fuck. I slapped a hand to my chest, my heart beating hard enough to break. It was breaking. I was breaking.

Tarsier O.O: Is this a joke? It's not funny, Caleb. Where are you?

Tarsier O.O: Caleb?

Tarsier O.O: Please, come talk to me. We don't have to stay at the fair. Please come get me so we can talk.

Me: I can't. I'm sorry.

Her shoulders slumped forward and her face dropped, her hands immediately there to hide the tears she was crying. I choked on a sob of my own, unable to stop it. Dammit. Goddammit. Mer was talking in her ear, Jacob listening beside them and scanning the crowd. Celia shook her head and ducked into the line, escaping the few steps to be alone. But instead of standing still, she threw herself into the next bucket. Mer and Jacob didn't follow. They moved away from the line as Celia continued to go up higher and higher when more people got on. When she stopped at the top, I could barely see her head. Maybe the hurt would be over for her soon, I hoped. After all, she'd only recently chosen me. I'd chosen her long before, so I knew I was fucked.

Before her bucket moved again, she held up the daisy, cocked her arm back, and chucked it forward. It flipped petals over stem, over and over, disappearing into the darkness past the fair's perimeter fence.

23
Celia

-now-

"I know, Jerry," I replied, raising my eyebrows at Caleb as he opened the door to his house. Our phones had been dead when we left, so I didn't call work while still at the quarry. I also didn't want to call in the truck because Jerry would listen to everything on my end, analyzing every sound. He'd done it before when I called in sick from my couch, asking if I was on a beach somewhere drinking a cocktail after hearing my TV in the background. Only now, he'd kinda be right, except that I'd just left a little wanna-be beach and the drink was a tall glass of Caleb.

"And you're still on watch." Jerry's snappy voice was loud enough for me to jerk the phone away from my ear.

"I know, Jerry," I repeated, looking around Caleb's place. It was a basic layout. Single room. Much like my apartment in size, though more boxy than long. Living area up front. Kitchen along the side. Bathroom and bedroom at the back. And plenty of windows, all with gray curtains and white doily valances. I smiled, knowing that the wife of the Mennonite farmer had likely decorated and made it all herself. Except for the wooden dining set and a couple accent chairs. Those were Caleb. The kitchen had a small three-burner stove and a fridge that was also smaller than the norm.

Caleb walked past, exaggerating his careful steps and lifting an eyebrow. I bit my lip with a smile. He disappeared into the bathroom and shut the door.

"So this will be only one day without pay," Jerry continued.

"Yes. Could be something I ate." There weren't many pictures. The bookshelf beside the fireplace had a few of their family. One of him and Mer at his high school graduation.

"All right then. We will see you tomorrow."

"Yes. Thanks, Jerry."

No "feel better soon" from him, no way. Jerk.

Caleb walked out of the bathroom and started unloading the extra water and ice packs from the cooler. "Everything go all right?"

"Hmm," I replied with pressed lips, stepping beside him.

"That bad, huh?"

"Yeah, well, I can't really be mad about it since I'm lying."

"You can if it's been the same even when you haven't lied."

"True," I agreed, focusing on his veined hands and forearms, and also the flex in his biceps as he moved around. "Need help with anything?"

He ran a palm over his head, brushing back the thick longer hair above that was just shy of reaching his eyes when wet. "Nope. I only need to send a message to Jay and Sam so they're prepared for another possible video. Hey," he added, the corner of his lips pulling into a cute smile. "You interested in sending them some of the shots you took too? They might consider using them."

"Yeah, sure. Let me grab my memory card."

"I'll pull a few." He disappeared into his room, and I followed after grabbing the camera.

The space was simple like the rest of the house. Queen bed with tan pillowcases and covers and a rustic plank headboard. There was a dresser and chair to match, all carved intricately along the edging.

"These are beautiful." I ran a finger along the top of the dresser. There was no need to ask if he'd made them. Celtic knots were the designs along the edges, something he favored.

"Thanks," he replied, taking a seat at his desk and opening his email.

I handed over the memory card, catching sight of a picture beside his monitor of Mer and me. It was the graduation picture from her room. I coughed a little, choked up by the memories and that he'd brought it home and kept it so close.

He eyed me, noticing what I'd seen. Without a word, he stood again, palming my cheeks and kissing me, knowing I needed that contact. He pressed his forehead to mine. "I'll make us some food after I get this sent. Do you need or want anything?"

"A shower?" I tugged on the ends of my hair, which was stiff from all the swimming.

"Of course. Soap, shampoo, and towels are in the bathroom."

"Thanks."

I wasted no time jumping into the claw-footed tub, drawing the translucent curtain around the circular rod suspended above the standing shower pipe. It was only after I was already wet that I realized all his soap was on the vanity sink.

"Uhh," I said out loud. A knock followed moments later. "Help, I forgot the soap."

His laughter came from behind the door before it opened

and his blurry form appeared. "And here I was struggling to come up with any reason to get in here."

I peeked my face out of the curtain then thought better of it and pulled it open, leaving only a section closed to contain the water. "You don't need a reason."

"So glad for that," he replied, handing over the soap and shampoo as his eyes roamed down my body. He licked his lips.

"You gonna help me?" I offered.

"Yes." He nodded with a grin. "Fuck yes, I will."

I giggled as he stripped and nearly tripped over his shorts climbing into the tub. Drawing the curtain closed again, I watched the water hit him and glide down the sexy lines and curves of his muscular body. I lifted my hands to his chest, rubbing gently.

"Uh-uh. You first." He brushed a quick kiss to my lips then turned me around and adjusted the water. His fingers pushed into my hair, soaping and massaging. A cloth was next, slathering suds on my shoulders and back then moving around my front, up my neck and down to my breasts. He was hard against the top of my ass, and I sighed, feeling every bit as turned on as him. He slid his hands around again, rubbing over my ass cheeks then to my thighs. He guided me into a turn and fell into a squat, washing the front of my legs and slipping a hand in between. His eyes peered up to mine as his fingers stroked against me.

I sighed again, bit my lip, and tilted my face to the ceiling. The feeling was maddening, making me so hot. I needed more but wanted to take care of him first. "Your turn." I rinsed my hair as he stood, then dumped some shampoo into my palm. "Your hair has darkened so much over the years. And when it's wet like this, it's practically brown."

His only reply was a contented hum as I massaged his

wet strands as best as I could with his head tipped backward. I grabbed the washcloth from his hand, added more soap, and started over his broad shoulders and back, following the taper down his waist, over his round ass. I may have stayed there longer than needed because he started to laugh. After his thighs, I stood and let him turn so I could wash down his front. He was so solid, his muscles tightening even more as I moved my hands over them. I worked quickly down his thighs and calves then climbed back up, rubbing the cloth over his balls first, watching him as he had done to me, enjoying the soft breath he released as he tipped his head back. Sliding farther, I stroked up his length, gripping firmly.

"I need you. Right now," he said, grabbing the handheld part of the shower and rinsing my body of soap before spinning it on himself. I couldn't pry my eyes away from him and what could only be described as the shower show of my dreams, the heat between my legs building.

Instead of waiting, I fell to my knees, grabbed hold, and took him into my mouth.

"Fuck," he said with a grunt. His face tipped down as I looked up and continued to suck him. He dropped the showerhead, and it clanked against the tub beside me. Water dripped down the longer strands of his hair, falling down to meet my face, my eyes. I blinked, and within a few seconds, he pulled away from my hold, turned off the water, and helped me out of the tub.

"We're still wet!" I laughed as he hauled me into his arms. My hands locked into a death grip around his neck, trying my best to maintain some control as our slick bodies slid against each other.

"I'm not waiting to dry off," he said, slaloming the doorways to get into his bedroom. His feet slipped on the hardwood, and I squeaked with fright as we toppled backward and slammed to the ground. "Oof."

"Oh my God." My words were broken between giggles. My body vibrated on top of his, but I couldn't move if I wanted to. His arms had me pinned against him securely.

He thunked his head back against the floor and laughed. "Maybe I should have waited."

"Aw." I wriggled out of his hold then leaned over and kissed his smiling mouth. "Anything broken?"

He lifted his head and glanced downward at his still very hard dick. "Nope. I'm good."

I rolled my eyes with a smile. Before I could even reply, he hopped up onto his feet and yanked me with him, pinning my body close and slamming his mouth to mine. I wrapped my hands around the back of his neck and melted into him as he guided us the rest of the way into the bedroom.

A loud tone beeped somewhere at the front of the house. My phone.

He backed away from my lips. "You need to get that?"

"No. Absolutely not."

"Good," he replied, sliding his hands down to my ass, squeezing firmly, lifting me, and tossing me onto his bed.

I was stunned by the disconnection of our mouths for a moment, my lips still parted as I fell back onto my elbows.

He crawled up and leaned in to kiss me one more time before his mouth moved to my neck, licking a trail with his tongue to follow the prickly scratches from his scruffy chin. My breasts were next. His hand smoothed over the skin, stroking softly before rolling my pebbled nipple between his fingers. His mouth took the other in, his tongue swirling before he nipped a bite.

"Ah." I kicked my head back as delicious tingles rippled over my body.

"I never thought I'd ever see you like this, taste you like this," he whispered to my skin while traveling down, down, down. His hands parted my legs farther, spreading me wide, gripping my thighs as he propped them up. He hummed as he lowered his mouth to me, kissing chastely, and digging his fingers into my skin.

As soon as his tongue licked a full stroke, my arms buckled and I fell onto my back, pinching my eyes closed and gripping the comforter.

Heaven. It was heaven. And he made me feel like a goddess, worshiping me so reverently.

"So good," I murmured then exhaled his name in praise.

He didn't stop, only gripped me harder, kissing and flicking his tongue then pushing it inside. I moaned when I felt his finger enter, curling and stroking.

His rhythm was magic, building me up, higher and higher. I gasped and panted, feeling every bit of the connection. And then I came apart at all seams, whimpering in short bursts as an orgasm rocked me.

"I think I see stars," I said, my eyes closed tightly, watching the flashes of light behind my lids. "You made me see stars."

His warm chuckle reached my ears. I wasn't sure how since my focus had been entirely on feeling for several minutes.

"That was beautiful," he whispered, pressing his lips to my belly button. "You are beautiful and so damn sexy. I promise you'll see those stars often enough to name them."

"I like that idea," I admitted, slipping my fingers into his damp hair. "Right now, I want you to see them too."

24
Caleb

-now-

She was on my lips. In my nose. Under my skin. Everywhere I'd dreamed of having her. And she tasted as divine as I knew she would, and now, like a fiend, I only wanted more. I was prepared to give her everything, dine on her over and over again, content to ignore my own need for release if it meant I got to keep pleasuring her, loving her.

She leaned up, captured my face with her hands, then my lips with her own. "I need you inside me." Her hands pulled at my face, urging me farther up onto the bed before shoving my body over.

I rolled onto my back with what was probably the most dumbstruck and goofiest grin on my face ever. Thank God I didn't have a mirror on the ceiling. Actually … Right now, as she leaned over my body, kissing and licking my stomach, I was wishing I did have one to see her at every angle, to see our connection from another viewpoint. Thinking about it got me harder. Damn.

"I have to grab a condom."

"Where?" she asked, grazing her teeth along my skin.

"Desk. Side drawer."

She jumped off the bed, and I leaned up on my elbows, watching her bend over as she looked inside the drawer, her ass sticking out with a lovely glisten at the apex between her legs. I licked my lips.

When she spun around and climbed back onto the bed, she tossed the condom onto my chest. "Open that, please."

I grabbed the wrapper, ready to obey, but she had other plans.

She took hold of me again as she had in the shower, cupped my balls, then slid her mouth over me.

My body jerked in response, overloaded by the sensation. "Ah. Damn." The words were caught in my throat.

She stroked me, twisting as she sucked. So hot. So wet. When her eyes peered up at me, looking through her lashes, I had to rein myself in. "Celia. Oh. This will bring the stars. But please," I begged, not wanting to explode.

She giggled and the vibration nearly pushed me too far. With one more lick and a kiss, she held out her hand for the condom, which I'd forgotten entirely about. She laughed again as I ripped that fucker open in record speed. Her fingers worked, rolling it down onto me. I sat up, ready to go, but she shoved me back down and climbed over my legs, straddling me.

"And now you've fulfilled my wildest dream," I said, reaching up to her breasts, massaging as she leaned forward and took hold.

"Am I? What exactly did you dream about?" she asked, positioning me and sitting down slowly.

I gritted my teeth and released a long breath, the feeling so good it hurt. "This. You. I used to lie in bed …" She pushed down more until she was fully seated, her big, glorious eyes watching me as I panted.

"And?" she prompted.

"I'd picture you sneaking out of Mer's room at night and coming into mine."

"Oh, did you?" She rocked forward, sliding herself up.

"Fuck yes, I did. My God. You'd crawl into my bed ... we'd kiss ..."

"Did you touch yourself then? Thinking of me?" She sat down, painfully slow.

My eyes rolled into the back of my head as my brain homed in on every single nerve receptor in my dick. "Yes." I admitted, thinking of all the times. Innumerable. Uncountable times. Wanting her.

She exhaled a sigh and was leaning up again for another stroke, arching her back, pushing her breasts harder into my hands. "I thought of coming to you, not long after the fair, still wanting you."

"Fuck," I said with a groan, every muscle in my body tight with anticipation.

"I touched myself for you, too. Thinking of your kisses. Your body against mine." She pumped faster and rolled her hips.

I almost lost my mind at her truth, at the feeling of it all. I dropped a hand and slipped my fingers over her, rubbing where my tongue had been.

"Ahh." She tipped her face back and bounced harder.

I bucked my hips from below, finding her rhythm, gripping her waist to slam her back down onto me as her need grew.

She released that wonderful breathy whimpering melody as she came.

I waited only a moment before flipping her onto her back

then kissing her as I entered her again. Her fingernails dug into my skin, and she moaned. "Oh yes. Wanna go again?"

"I … Oh, that's so good."

I quickened my pace and grabbed hold of the headboard for leverage. Her phone rang again out in the living room. "Not happening," I murmured.

She giggled until I thrust inside her, bringing out a louder moan. "Caleb."

"Yes, baby." Sweat broke through my skin as my body sped up. Leaning down, I kissed her neck then bit down softly, anchoring myself.

"Oh, oh, oh." Her body shook, her head tipped back, and her eyes clamped tight.

The sight and sound of her orgasm was enough to make me lose what little control I had left. I moaned and closed my eyes as the pleasure pulsed from me. My body stilled and sagged against hers. It was too much. She was too much. "I'm thinking I might be seeing those stars too."

Her breathy laugh drew my eyes open. "So good."

"So good," I echoed, staring at her, wanting to memorize how she looked. With flushed, glowing skin, and wet hair spread over my pillow. "This look. It's even better than your morning look." She smiled brightly, not a hint of shyness or doubt. I kissed those smiling lips and pulled away fully to tie and toss the condom before collapsing onto my back.

She tucked in, draping her limbs over me. "I think this is my favorite look of yours too."

"Oh yeah? The 'I just had the best sex of my life with the woman of my dreams' look?"

Her fingers roamed my chest, drawing circles. "No, the dreamy and sated and 'I just gave her a few orgasms' look."

"Hell yeah. Better get used to seeing it all the time." My phone beeped a message from the desk. "No," I protested. "I don't want to leave this bed."

"I do," she said, and I turned my face to see her, preparing to hold her captive if I needed to. "I'm starving."

"Oh, good point. You can stay. I'll make some food."

"No, I should probably get up too. Check my phone."

I kissed her forehead then kicked my feet onto the floor. "I can grab you something clean to wear if you want."

"That sounds great, thanks."

She padded behind me to the dresser, and I grabbed a pair of sweat shorts for both of us and a T-shirt for her. As she started dressing, I checked my phone. "It's a text from Jay and Sam. They need to talk. Mind if I call them?"

"No, go ahead."

I hit the call button and put it on speaker while I made my way into the kitchen.

After a single ring, Sam answered, "Hey, Caleb."

"Sam. You got the email then? Did you see Celia's pictures?"

"Oh … yeah. They're really great. She's talented. If she wants us to use them, she'll have to sign a different release form for those. I can email it to you."

"Great!" I looked at Celia and pointed toward the phone while I loaded the Keurig. She smiled, walking over to the counter to stand beside me. "I have you on speaker too, by the way. She's here with me."

"Cool. Yes, great job with those shots. If you want to talk shop, maybe send us some of the rest of your portfolio too, Celia."

"That's great. Thank you." She raised her eyebrows and smiled big at the news and also at the mug of coffee I handed over. She prepped hers with cream and sugar while I made a cup for myself.

"So yeah, I'm glad you're both there," Sam continued. "Listen, the guy who used to work with us and Merilyn. Vince. He's the one behind the videos, we know that. And he did put another one up about an hour or so ago."

"Shit. Will you be able to get it down?" I asked, finishing my coffee prep and taking a sip while I watched Celia do the same.

"We have a bigger problem than before. Um. This went big. Really quick. It's because it's not his footage, it's ours— well, yours. Everything you shot. Plus pictures of the notebook worked in as well."

"What?!" Celia said, her eyes popping wide while I almost choked on my coffee.

Still coughing, I said, "No way. He didn't take the GoPro." Celia darted over to the table where it sat, and that was when it hit me too. "I didn't check the memory card."

Celia opened the camera casing right as Sam confirmed, "He has it all."

"Dammit. Shit." Every muscle in my body clenched, and the urge to throw my mug was almost too strong to control. "I'm sorry. I screwed that up. I should have downloaded all the footage before." I set my mug down and ran my hands over my face, feeling as if the world had crash-landed on top of me. I'd let Mer down, let Celia down.

"Yeah, well, he gave Merilyn's followers exactly what we wanted to give them. Only it's a sloppy job. Unedited. Everything you filmed is up there. We're waiting for Adventure Life to return our calls about copyright infringement so we can get it taken down as well as obtain all the footage since it's legally ours. And we've had our lawyer send Vince a cease and desist also."

"Everything," Celia murmured, realizing the full extent. All of it was out there right now with who knew how many people watching. "I feel a little sick." She sat down on my couch.

"I'm really sorry this has happened, too," Sam said. "Obtaining the video shouldn't be too difficult, even if he destroys the SD card. We'll still be able to move on with this tribute to her. As soon as we can do that, we'll also settle all payments."

"What?" Celia whispered. "Payments?" Her eyes flitted from me to a spot on the floor, chewing on her lower lip.

"In the meantime, do whatever you have left. We'll put it all together in the end. Try not to worry too much."

"All right, Sam. Talk to you later." I ended the call and looked at Celia.

"He said—" Her phone went off again. "Caleb, they're paying you for this? And what did he mean when he said 'he gave the followers what we wanted to give them'? I thought you said this was Mer's last request."

"The list was her final request," I said with a nod. "But Jay and Sam knew about it and approached me about filming."

"You said it was to give her followers closure, not for money." Her phone went off again. She eyed it as she stood up then cut her glare back to me.

"It was—is meant to give closure. It's why I agreed to do it. The money was just—"

"Padding for your pockets?"

"It's not like that," I said, shaking my head.

"Then why didn't you tell me?"

"I didn't think it was important—"

"You let me believe that it was for Mer. That she wanted it filmed. It's because you thought I wouldn't have agreed to do it otherwise, isn't it?"

"No, that's not …" I pushed off the counter and moved to her, touching her upper arms gently. She crossed them over her chest, setting a barrier between us, but stayed still. "After what happened back then, and at the wake, I thought knowing Mer wanted us to do the list was the most important thing to tell you. I didn't think the other stuff was necessary."

"No? Really? So you leave off information that is essential to me making an actual decision. This sounds like another time …"

"What? No, this is nothing like that, Celia. Please, listen. I wasn't trying to deceive you."

"And the money? What the hell is that? You profit off your sister's death?"

Anger flared at the accusation, and I huffed a harsh breath to keep my reaction in check. "I knew her followers might need closure, might need to go through the list with us, to heal. I have no platform and no skill when it comes to that stuff. There was no way I'd do it justice if I'd wanted to do it myself. They offered to handle it, since they are technically still part of her channel, even though their contracts will dissolve because of her death. I agreed on terms they worked out with Adventure Life about handling the channel, for them to get compensated for their work too. Half of my portion is yours. The rest will be used for the family business since she left some of her own money for that as well, after most was donated to charity. So please don't accuse me of using my sister's death for profit."

She blinked at me, disdain still very much alive in her hard-ened stare. Her phone went off again, and she moved to answer it.

"Nadine, can I call you ba—what? What do you mean?" She paced around in a circle and bit on her thumbnail. "You're serious? He saw it?" A sob burst through her lips, and I was instantly at her side, knowing something was wrong and wanting to comfort her, though I doubted she wanted me there at that moment. "Yeah. No, it's not your fault. It's mine. Thank you for calling. I'll see you."

I watched her for a few silent moments, waiting. "Celia?"

She nodded solemnly at the floor. "I just got fired." Her lips pressed together and she seemed to snap out of a trance, moving around the space, stuffing her phone into her clothes bag then grabbing her camera bag too.

"What? Why?"

"My floor supervisor, my boss, watched that latest video. It seems it was as widespread as Sam said. So imagine his surprise when he sees me skinny-dipping in the quarry instead of throwing my guts up in my apartment."

"Fuck," I murmured.

"Yeah. Fuck." She slung her bags over a shoulder and clenched her keys.

"Wait, Celia. There has to be something—"

"There's nothing, Caleb. Nothing right now. I now have to figure out how I'm going to make rent and bills ... I don't ... I can't ..." She spun around, making sure she had everything.

"Look, this could be a good thing, right? Maybe it all happens for a reason."

She laughed, shrill and cold. "I'm not ignoring my fault in this. I made the choice to stay last night. But since you wanted to know yesterday what you could give me ... give me my job back, Caleb. Erase these last few days and give me my life back so I don't have to go hunt for a new job."

"Celia—"

"I've gotta go."

"I'm sorry." The words came out right before the door closed. I couldn't take it all back, but I would do anything to fix it.

25

Celia

-now-

I hadn't had the courage to go to the office in the middle of the day. Facing everyone there, knowing they had likely watched the video, seen what I'd done. It felt a little too crushing. The video was embarrassing enough. Then tack on my spectacular lie …

What a cruel joke it seemed to be. I knew Mer would have been pissed off too. She would have called Caleb an ass again, for the one thousand ninety-first time. How could I have been so stupid?

I stared at my reflection in Pearson Insurance's glass entrance doors. Most people would be gone after close of normal business. No new clients to write in and no payroll tweaking after six. File clerks could still be around if they were able to land the overtime. Of course, Jerry and some other supervisors would be around too.

When I shuffled onto my floor and headed to my desk to collect my stuff, Jerry emerged from his office—plaid tie loose, brittle comb-over sticking up. Without a single word, he placed a payroll envelope and an official letter of termination on my desk. His eyes flicked to me in a dead stare then he was off, walking a little crooked as if the weight of the day was a hundred pound brick inside his briefcase. He wasn't even the one getting fired.

"Well, fuck you too, Jerry!" I called after him, no longer giving a shit. Funny how that happened when the dam broke. "I lied one time. One time! I worked hard for this place, and all you did was treat me like a piece of shit on a shoe. Well, you know what? I hope … I hope you …" I exhaled a deep breath, the anger deflating out of me. Fuck.

To his credit, he never turned and never flinched. But really, I didn't care, and he likely didn't either. He'd had to fire people before, and I was certain he'd heard much worse than I'd managed to spit out. It was a waste of breath.

I looked around one more time and decided that Caleb was right, even if I was pissed at him. It all happened for a reason. As I walked back to my car, I pictured Mer there waiting, leaning a cocked hip against my beat-up Civic, long hair blowing over her shoulder as she nodded in agreement. Slipping into my seat, I let my head fall to the wheel and my tears fall down my cheeks.

Minutes or maybe hours later, my phone beeped. Text. Caleb had tried to call and text earlier but seemed to have given up for the day, realizing I wouldn't reply. And even though I was conflicted on the idea of seeing his name again, I looked.

Nadine: You all right?

Me: Yeah. Got my final check. Headed home.

Nadine: The ladies rallied for you today. They beat Jerry up about it.

Me: He looked it.

Nadine: I think word of the revolt traveled upstairs.

Me: Doubtful.

Nadine: Not from what I saw. And did you watch the video?
Me: No.

And I likely never would. I didn't even want to think about what was on it. None of it was edited. The fact that it was stolen was bad enough, but the tribute to Mer being seen so roughly had my stomach knotted. He'd even showed pictures of the notebook. And then there was the other part of it, all the personal stuff Caleb and I had shared. Everything we'd said. Everything we'd done. I shook my head. I couldn't watch it.

Nadine: I understand that you are upset, but you need to see what we saw, what thousands of people have seen.

Me: Please stop. That's not helping right now.

Nadine: Come out with us tomorrow night. I think you need a night.

Me: Tomorrow's Tuesday.

Nadine: Schedules are cleared. Husbands and sitters are on duty.

I smiled sadly at the phone, knowing that it would possibly be one of the last regularly scheduled nights with them. There was no telling how much free time I'd have at whatever job I got, what shift I'd work.

Me: Okay.

26
Caleb

-now-

"Yeah, I'm here to see a Jerry. I'm sorry, I don't have his last name."

The young receptionist plucked the phone up with her talon nails and murmured into the receiver, eyeing me curiously.

"Is that him?" A distant whisper hit my ears as I slid my fingers along the waistband of my pants, adjusting the tuck of my button-down.

It was nine in the morning, and I was already sweating. After driving two hours and stressing, it was no wonder. Luckily, that stress had nothing to do with my own job. My father had no issue with me taking off again to right my wrong. My stress was all about Celia and if I could get her job back, whether she'd give me another chance or not.

I looked around the stuffy lobby of Pearson Insurance. Fake ficus. Pressed wood desks and flimsy plastic chairs. Vivid abstract canvases meant to liven up an otherwise drab place and only having an adverse effect by calling attention to the stark difference.

I had to wonder what was so appealing about the place. But I checked myself again, knowing that it wasn't my choice. If Celia wanted the job back, was content with it, I would try my hardest to make that happen. It was my fault. I was to blame for all of it.

"It is him," another voice said.

I turned my head the other way, catching the eyes of two women in the doorway of a break room, a table and chairs set up behind them. The curly brunette crossed her arms, and the blonde whipped out her phone, typing furiously. They didn't look away, so feeling the awkwardness creep in, I turned back to the receptionist.

"He's finishing with a meeting upstairs. He'll be down in a moment. You can have a seat if you want," she said, smiling brightly and flicking her black hair over a shoulder.

"Uh-uh, honey," the curly-haired woman at the break room said with a glare aimed at her.

I let out a breath and took a seat close to the front door, trying my best to ignore what was happening. Celia had said that her coworkers had seen the video, which outed her sick day lie. So they obviously knew who I was, making this situation even more strange.

Noticing movement by the desk, I glanced over and saw the dark-haired guy who had been at Celia's apartment. The BMW driver.

"Morning, Brent," the receptionist said with a giggly voice.

I gritted my teeth and forced my body to remain seated, suddenly losing all motivation to plead for Celia's job. Did I want her to work here with him? Hell no. But was it my choice? Fuck. That answer was also a no.

As his eyes cut to me and flashed with recognition, an older woman with a mass of braids wrapped at the crown of her head and flowing floor-length skirt appeared, hip checking the backside of Brent, shoving his bent body against the desk.

"Caleb," she said, her voice gentle as she continued to walk toward me, as if she'd known me for years.

Nadine. Celia and I had talked about several things on the short drive back to my house from the quarry. Times in college. Goals in life. But mostly friends. Nadine seemed to be the one who she was closest with. Also the one who had called to break the news the previous morning.

"Nadine," I replied. "I was told to thank you and a few others whenever I met you, for helping to convince Celia to speak to me again."

"Oh, right." She nodded with a genuine smile.

"Not sure if she'd still feel the same about that now. But I do. I owe you." When she didn't reply, only looked me up and down with a lifted brow, I added, "You gonna kick my ass?"

She chuckled and bit her smile, shaking her head. "No, honey. I had to meet you since you showed up here. Why are you here?"

"She doesn't deserve to be fired for my mistake. I want to try and make things right for her. Get her job back."

"Kinda hard to get your job back when you tell your supervisor to fuck off, though," she replied, widening her eyes and folding her hands together.

I let out a stiff breath. "Well, this could be more of a challenge than I thought."

"Might not even be necessary, actually." She looked over her shoulder at the two—now three other women in the break room doorway. "Anyway, as her friend, I'm obligated to tell her about your visit when we meet up with her later tonight."

"I wouldn't assume otherwise."

"And," she continued, "as her friend, I also plan on advising her to get her head out of her ass, as I have before."

"Nadine," a guy interrupted as he approached us.

"Jerry. Things go all right upstairs? You look like you've been wrung out a little," she replied in a bored tone with a lift of her eyebrows then turned her attention back to me. "I suppose your plan for the fair is still on for Friday evening, correct?"

I scrunched my brows then realized she'd seen the leaked video too, which had Celia and I discussing plans for the Ferris wheel task. "Yeah. I'm still going."

"Good," she said, eyeing Jerry again before walking off.

"Hi, Jerry. I'm Caleb." I extended a hand with a big smile, unable to shake off the hope Nadine had been able to plant inside me.

The balding guy took and shook but didn't offer a greeting at all. *All right then.*

"Look, I don't want to waste your time. You seem like a busy guy. I came here to ask you to reconsider Celia's job. I realize that she did lie, but she wouldn't have if it weren't for me. She was prepared to work, and I convinced her not to. I know it's probably odd for someone to come here and plead for another person's job, but I feel like I owe her this much after causing it to happen. Please know that she thinks highly of this company and still would love to continue to work here. I'm positive she won't repeat the same mistake."

He blinked at me.

"Is there any chance that she can get her position back?"

"It's not my call. Unfortunately," he tacked on the last word in a huff.

"So whose is it? Would I be able to speak with them?"

"No, it's not your concern. It's already been decided. Now,

if that's all …" He turned sharply and stalked off, not bothering to wait for my reply.

All three of the women standing near the break room waved at me. As Jerry passed by mumbling something, they all scattered down the back hallway.

I had no other cards to play. Celia refused to answer my calls, but I'd at least told her my intentions in a voicemail. Contacting the bosses after that would be crossing too big of a line. The company would either reconsider or they wouldn't, even without my attempt to push myself into the situation.

The only fight I had left was the one to get her back.

27

Celia

-now-

"Y ou beat us here," Nadine said, sliding into the booth beside me and wrapping me into her arms with a squishy booby hug. She eyed the half-empty margarita. "How many of those have you had?"

"This is the second," I admitted with a grin.

"Hey, girl," Mina, Deandra, and Julie said, or at least a variation of the same greeting as they slid into the booth across from us.

"Hi," I replied, then took a large gulp of my 'rita.

Their eyes stayed on me the entire time, watching, and their mouths remained closed. Eerie.

"Okay, what's with the eyes? I've been getting enough of that from the bartender. And maybe a few other people. I don't want my besties being creepy too. Speaking of," I added when the waiter came strutting over to our favorite bar section table.

"Ladies. What are we having tonight?"

"Four more margaritas," Julie said without even looking up at him.

"Five," I corrected, and Nadine elbowed my arm. "What? I Ubered here."

"Okay, you need to spill," Julie urged while Mina glanced around, running her fingers through her hair, hoping to catch some eyes. I knew I could count on her to make the hunt for dick more important than what was happening in my life. The other three … not so much.

"About what?"

"Don't play," Julie replied with an exaggerated sigh. "We saw—"

"Nope, we're not starting there," Nadine cut in, halting Julie's conversation direction. "We're starting with work. Did you get a phone call? Because I heard you were getting one."

"Yeah," Deandra added, propping her elbows onto the table and resting her chin on her hands. "It was obvious that Jerry had been thoroughly worked upstairs because he was like a limp noodle all day. It was fantastic."

The others nodded.

"Yeah, I got a call."

Nadine lifted her brows. "I know you aren't holding out right now."

"Fine." I adjusted my ass in the indent I'd created in the booth cushion, as if delaying my words would help me come up with an answer I hadn't come up with all day. "They said that they believed in second chances. That I was an important employee. And that they hoped I would consider their offer."

"What did they offer?" Nadine asked.

"They offered me an underwriting clerk position with a dollar raise and an opportunity for courses in the future should I want to progress further, go for my license."

"Attagirl! They better give you to me," Nadine said. "I assess the most clients and could use the help."

"That's amazing," Mina chimed in, genuinely looking at me for longer than a second. "The test is hard, though. And the studying is like—"

"Really?" Nadine said to her, tilting her head. "Let's not worry about all that nonsense yet. Plus, Celia is smart. She'll pass that on her first try. Not like some bitches I know."

Mina scoffed, and the others laughed. I tipped back drink number two to finish it off, which didn't go unnoticed.

"Something's still up," Nadine said, her tone quieting.

"I'm not sure anymore, ya know?" The waiter came back with the new drinks and I started in on mine, aiming to keep the hefty buzz I was rocking.

"It took the firing to really kick you in your ass, huh?" Julie said with a nod before taking a huge gulp of her drink.

"That and …"

"Caleb," Nadine finished.

"It's just … he said some stuff about jobs that …"

"Oh, girl, we know," Deandra said, her motherly eyes blinking at me.

"What? Oh, right." The video. "Fuck my life."

"So, yes, we agree. The offer is nice, but will you be happy?"

"I don't know anymore. I have to think about it."

"You also need to think about Caleb," Nadine added, licking a section of salt from her glass before taking the first sip.

"Are we finally talking about him?" Julie said with a big grin. "Goodie. Ooh, Celia. He is even more handsome in person. It's not even everything that was going on in that video, but the fact that he showed up today to try and get your job back. Not that he helped. They'd already handed Jerry his ass first thing in the a.m."

"He did show up?" I asked, sinking into the booth a little. "He left a message, but I didn't think he'd …"

"Follow through?" Nadine asked sharply. "That boy fucking loves you, girl. If you can't see how serious he is, then you are blind, blind, blind."

"I see it, I do. I'm so upset about the video. He never told me that it wasn't part of Mer's request. She only wanted us to do the list. There was nothing about filming it and posting it to her channel."

"But wasn't he doing it for her followers, for them to have some closure too? That's what you explained before." Nadine's voice was softer, thoughtful.

"Yes, that's true. I … I don't know what to think."

"There's nothing to think. You really should watch the video," she replied as if it were the end-all.

"She can't now," Julie said. "I checked before leaving work. It was removed."

"Oh, thank God," I murmured, closing my eyes. "They were able to get it down." I took another drink, celebrating that relief.

"Not until after about a hundred thousand views," Julie added.

After a gasp, my lungs refused to inhale the margarita in my mouth, kicking me into a choking fit and spraying all remaining liquid across the table.

"Celia! Shit!" Mina screeched, wiping her face down with a napkin while the others threw more onto the table.

"I'm sorry, but what?" The words rushed out in a tipsy mumble.

"Yeah, I told you," Nadine said. "I doubt it was only Merilyn's followers hooked on that video. And I'm certain that everyone, including us, will be anxiously awaiting the next one with all the edits, eager to see the rest of the tasks you need to complete, places to visit with your touching tributes, and of course to witness the incredible love story."

"Love story?" I squeaked as I wiped my chin.

"That's why it blew up," Deandra said with a nod. "What you two have ... It was fantastic to watch."

"Yes," Nadine agreed. "So even though you need to work through your own shit, you also need to accept the fact that he is perfect for you."

"And this is coming from you, Ms. Anti-Love?" I asked, shooting her a side-eye.

"I'm not anti-love. I'm anti-bullshit. There's a huge difference. And he is no bullshit. He neglected to tell you something. He told you he didn't mean to deceive you. Do you believe him?"

I bit my lips together thinking of the fight I'd had with Caleb, considering all that we had done. "Yes. I think I do."

"Well, then, your butt needs to tell him. Preferably sooner than later."

"I ... I need some time."

"You have about three days because Friday night you will be at that fair and on that Ferris wheel, even if I need to pump you full of margaritas first."

"How do I know if—"

"He'll be there," she said then took a sip of her drink with a smile still on her lips.

Caleb

-now-

The fair was packed with cars and bodies. I almost wanted to bail, call Celia and postpone. When we'd discussed coming on opening night, I hadn't thought much about how crowded it would be. At that point, our focus was completing the tasks. But I should have known. Springtime fun. The end of school nearing for every district in the area. Prom season. It all brought back so many memories. Most of them good. Though as I looked across the fair at the Ferris wheel, its carts spinning around, reflecting the rays of the setting sun, I was hit with the one that haunted me the most. The biggest fucking regret of my life.

My calls and texts to Celia through the week remained unanswered, much like the calls and texts she'd made to me years before. I hated the thought of her choosing to move on. And while I flat out refused to give up on the idea of us after our time together, I also decided not to push her. I wouldn't become a psycho, even though I understood how easily it could happen for her. The last text I'd sent was the day before, letting her know my plans for tonight, that I'd continue the tasks for Mer as promised. I could only hope she'd show too.

Strapping the ticket band to my wrist and eyeing the setting sun, I realized I'd never mentioned a specific time. But if she hadn't arrived already, I'd gladly wait all night.

I trekked toward the Ferris wheel. No sense waiting anywhere else. Keeping Mer's urn clutched like a football in my arm, holding a single daisy in my other hand, with the notebook tucked in my back pocket and the GoPro—with a new memory card—stashed inside the front, I navigated around the carousel and kiddie rides, past the haunted mansion, and along the side row of game booths. The Ferris wheel stood at the far end of the lot as it had most years. Lights were already on, seeming to grow brighter as the sun dipped farther behind the treetops in the distance. A mix of rock and rap blared from the speakers of other rides while melodic accordion notes sounded from the carnival games. The smell of funnel cake and burgers would ordinarily have my stomach begging for sustenance, but tonight it only twisted my insides that much more.

The memory of Celia's face as she rode to the top alone flashed to mind as I stopped in the empty area in front and stared up at the wheel. Knowing it was possible I'd face the same fate tonight hurt beyond words. At least I knew what was coming, though. Celia hadn't known then. My heart felt as if it was breaking all over again. If anything, the situation seemed the perfect punishment for my past actions and choices, even if I'd already suffered. Karma, right? What goes around …

"Hey, look. It's him," a female voice yelled somewhere close.

"Oh my God, it is!" another person replied, and a string of giggles followed.

Preparing to post myself at the base of the wheel to wait,

I glanced around to choose the best spot. Only, I was met with several stares from beside the ride's portable fence line. Turning my upper body, I checked behind me for the source of their attention, sure there was another person there. Nope.

"Caleb!" someone called out, and I twisted my head, seeking out a voice that wasn't Celia's but could've been someone else I knew. And that was another nope. The skinny middle school girl with braces smiled big and waved at me. I wracked my brain for a moment, wondering who her parents were, coming up short.

"Caleb, where's Celia?" another voice shouted.

That was when it all clicked. The video had been down for days, but Sam and Jay said it had made one helluva splash before it disappeared. Thousands. Like over a hundred thousand. In the back of my mind, I'd known about it, even thought about the impact of it during the week. What I hadn't considered, though, was other people showing up here, specifically because of the video, in order to see us.

"Shit," I murmured, keeping my face as neutral as possible. My eyes jumped all over, seeking an escape and finding no real options. I needed to stay and wait, but I wasn't exactly in the mood for this attention. It was weird.

More people seemed to gather, hearing my name, chatting with the others.

I hurried into the line, pressing a small smile for those who recognized me. Luckily, none had been daring enough to get close.

"Oh my gosh. And that's the urn. I can't believe we're seeing this. Record it. Record it. And look, he has a daisy," another person said, moving up behind me.

Annnd I'd thought too soon.

From the corner of my eye, I caught one posing with her back to me, holding up her phone to snap a selfie.

As the ride attendant loaded the next people in line, the last ones in front of me turned to stare. They were an older couple, blinking and clueless to what the growing commotion behind me was about. I let out a sigh. Small favors.

"The news is here," the middle school girl said.

What?

As the couple ahead of me made their way into the open bucket, I looked over my shoulder, watching in horror as a news reporter stalked toward the Ferris wheel with a wireless mic labeled Channel 2 in hand. A dude mostly hidden by a bulky camera trailed her closely.

I rushed up on the ride attendant, who was settling back behind his podium, pushing control buttons to spin the wheel.

"You gotta wait, man," he said, pointing a grease-stained finger to the streak of spray paint at the front of the fence line.

"Right. But I'm next, and I really need to get on that thing. Like right now. And stay on it." I glanced back over my shoulder right as the news chick spotted me. Her eyes bugged out, and she spun to the cameraman, her coiffed hair barely moving.

"Shit." I turned to the guy again, balancing everything in one arm as I wrenched my billfold out of my pocket. "I'm sure you don't take tips, but—"

"Oh, no, I definitely take tips."

"Great. I'll give you fifty right now if you put me on and leave me on for as long as I want. I'm waiting for someone. Another hundred comes to you when I'm done."

"You got it," he said, snatching the bills from me without hesitation.

"You gotta keep them back too. Don't let them too close to this area, all right?" I jerked my head over my shoulder to indicate the group of people following the news chick.

"Sure thing," he agreed as the bucket stopped.

I gritted my teeth, the seconds ticking by in my head as a set of kids crawled out of the seat, stumbling around in slow motion. Once they were clear, I hopped in that fucker faster than The Flash. Dude didn't even check the bar. He cranked the controls right up, taking me away from the crazy shit below, and I let out a relieved sigh.

"Caleb! Caleb Samuels," a voice called up. I glanced over the side, and the news chick waved, the camera behind her pointing up at me. "Are you here with Celia?"

More people stopped and gathered. I could almost see the change in the crowd as word spread. Wild.

After a while, I spaced out, watching the sun disappear completely, the lights flashing around me. I was grateful for the attendant, skipping my bucket over and over, much to the news crew and everyone else's dismay.

I kept checking the people. Some stayed, some left, the interest fading. And although I was hoping Celia would show, I almost wished it would be even later so she wasn't harassed by the circus below.

"Caleb!" a voice called out. Not Celia's. I was tempted to ignore it, but it sounded familiar. I peered over the edge and immediately saw a head of coiled braids and a wide, friendly smile shining under the colorful lights of the wheel.

When my bucket came around again, I yelled for the attendant to let Nadine closer. He stopped the ride and continued to play guard after he let her pass.

"Hey, there," she said, holding out a fountain drink and looking around at the people staring at us. "Thought you might be a bit thirsty. This guy mentioned that you've been spinning a while."

"Thanks," I replied, grabbing the drink and taking a sip.

"No drinks on the ride, man," the attendant said without turning.

Nadine scrunched her lips, threw a glare over her shoulder at him, then took the cup back from me.

"Do you know if she's coming?" I didn't want to be rude, but Celia was my only interest.

She shook her head. "I thought, maybe. But I haven't talked to her since Tuesday night."

"Okay. That's okay."

"Listen," she said as the attendant pushed the button again. She shot him another glare, and he shrugged. "We're staying here. Holler at me if you need something, honey." She pointed over to the side where the other women from Celia's work were standing, several kids running around them, a few boy-friends or husbands with arms full of snacks and stuffed toys.

"Yeah, I will. Thank you."

Numbness set in after that and a chill ran through me as the possibility of her not showing settled in, my body no longer warm with anticipation or hope. Maybe it was the end after all. I'd gotten just enough time with her to know how badly I'd love her for the rest of my life and never be able to have her again.

I wiped a hand down my face as the bucket moved upward, perching me at the top while another was reloading below. All I could do was tip my head back and look at the stars, letting the misery begin to take over as my mind drifted to the night at the quarry when I'd stared at the same stars with Celia in my arms.

A few whistles cut through the music and chatter below. And then cheers followed. The games. Someone was getting lucky, probably even more so later. I smiled sadly. When the cheers only grew louder, my mind flipped a switch and my heart began to pound.

"Celia!" The cheers blended into her name, voices echoing in a happy chorus that reached inside my body and set it on fire.

I popped the latch on the lap bar and stood up, scanning the crowd, seeing Nadine cutting a path through a mass of bodies.

When Celia's head tipped back, those big fucking eyes staring right up at me and locking on, I inhaled a huge breath, ignoring the sting in my sinuses as emotion kicked me harder than a shot to the nuts, nearly bringing the tears.

She came.

She smiled gorgeously and followed Nadine, who hip checked the news reporter.

I pushed those emotions back down, knowing that she could have shown up for Mer, to honor the request. And that was still a good thing. At least she came. I calmed myself with another breath and continued to watch her walk closer as my bucket started to move downward.

"Sit down, or I'm booting you and keeping your cash," the attendant called up to me.

"Right," I agreed in a stupor then yelled down, "She's with me."

"No shit," he replied, causing me to laugh.

I told myself I wouldn't lose my cool. Seeing her, talking to her—I would need all of my control to test where her head was at. Holding it together, that was the plan. Until she got close enough. Tight jeans with ripped holes along the legs. Baby blue Chucks on her feet. A lacy, fitted tank top that hugged her in all the ways I wanted to.

And pinched in her fingers, she held a wooden daisy.

My girl.

29
Celia

-now-

Deep breath. That was what I needed. Stepping foot onto the fairgrounds was like being slapped by the past. It was later. Dark. I should have texted Caleb, but I knew where he would be.

At first, everything seemed perfectly normal. A huge amount of people for the first night of the fair. Lights twinkling. Music roaring as the rides zipped around. Kids screaming. Closer to the Ferris wheel, I noticed a large crowd gathered as if they were standing in front of the performance stage instead.

"Celia! Look, it's her!" someone said. And suddenly heads were whipping around, bodies began to move, parting a small path.

"This is amazing!" a few girls off to my side yelled, hopping in place.

The crowd engulfed me quickly, and I kept moving forward, hoping I wouldn't get trampled. It was insanity. People pushed in close, some calling my name, others saying Caleb's. It was all because of the video and the most surreal thing I'd ever experienced. Had it really been that big?

"Hey, girl," Nadine's voice broke through them all.

"Oh my God, Nadine. You're here," I said, kissing her cheek as she appeared at my side, spreading her arms wide, blocking and leading the way.

"Are you kidding? We wouldn't have missed this for anything," she replied, winking then tipping her head toward the side of the Ferris wheel where Deandra, Mina, and Julie all stood waving, their younger kids running in circles around them.

"You guys are the best. Thank you."

"He's been waiting for you, babe," she said, glancing up as we continued on.

I looked up and saw him immediately, his tall body at the very top looking down with the biggest, sexiest smile.

"No exclusive tonight, darlin'," Nadine said to a blonde with a microphone, sticking her hip out and bumping the chick backward.

Holy shit. A reporter?

I spun the wooden daisy in my fingers, nerves on overload, and glanced up again in the final few steps. Caleb's bucket came to a stop at the bottom, and he hopped out to me.

"Get it, girl," Nadine said then backed away.

"Hi." The word was nearly lost in all the cheers of the crowd as I stepped up the ramp.

"Hi." His eyes did a full sweep of me. "You look so beautiful."

"Thank you." And he looked great too—clean-shaven, longer pieces of hair styled back in a messy wave.

"We better get on here before they attack."

"Yeah," I agreed, taking the hand he extended and letting him help me into the seat. He braced Mer's urn against the corner while I sat down.

The cheers grew louder as I watched him turn and thank

the attendant. The contours of his back and shoulders moved under his plain gray T-shirt, which was bunched up at the waist of the jeans, displaying his round ass nicely. Being here, seeing him ... my heart was melting once again.

People continued to cheer as Caleb sat down beside me and the wheel began to move. I glanced up, catching the eyes of the girls in the seat above us, only the top of their faces visible.

"This is unreal," he murmured, leaning back and looking down at the urn now in his hands.

"Very."

He reached to his side of the seat and pulled out a daisy I hadn't noticed before. I smiled as he handed it to me, thinking of all the times before.

His fingers gently touched the petals of the wooden daisy in my other hand, the one he'd made. "I thought you tossed this?"

"I—" Wait ... "Were you here that night?"

"Yeah, I was here. Knowing that I would cave if I got too close, I still felt I needed to be here to watch you through it, to face you without facing you, to not be a complete coward. It all seems so stupid now. I should have ignored Mer then. She thought she was doing what was best for you when really she was thinking about her own feelings. She was the one who needed to get away, to see the world, to experience it all. Maybe somehow she knew she didn't have much time ... But she was also projecting her dreams on you. She was afraid you wouldn't get the same chances. That was her final push for you, making sure I wasn't your anchor."

I swallowed the lump in my throat as I thought about that night, about him watching me from afar, about Mer. "She meant well, I guess."

A laugh burst from his lips and one bubbled up from me too. "Yeah, she did," he agreed.

"And, yes, I couldn't leave the daisy here. After I got off the ride, I went and found it. So glad all of it is in the past," I admitted, looking at the urn, wishing after everything that Mer was sitting with us instead. Deep down I knew I'd gladly relive it all again if she could too.

"Is it?" he asked, shifting in the seat to better face me, his eyes penetrating, needing the answer to a question filled with so much meaning. "I messed up. I should have told you every detail from the start. I also shouldn't have talked you into calling off work. That was dumb. Not that I regret spending more time with you because, damn, Celia, I can't get enough. I want every minute. I want it all. But after this week, I know you may not feel the same. And if that's what you want, I'll understand."

"It's not what I want," I breathed, laying my hand on his thigh. "I need to apologize too." When he shook his head, I continued, "Yes, I do. I'm sorry for accusing you of using her death for profit. That was horrible of me to say."

"It's all right. You were right to question it, to be upset."

"No, I completely overreacted. There was too much happening. I freaked out. I'm not used to so much. It was like my normal world had vanished in the span of a few minutes and it threw me into panic mode. But instead of reaching for you like I should have, I shoved you away and blamed you. That wasn't right. I am to blame for my own decisions, not you, so please don't feel my job was your fault. And I heard you went there for me, by the way."

"I did," he admitted, worry seeming to disappear from his body. His tense shoulders relaxed, his eyes softened, and his lips pulled up a little at the corners. "Didn't help, though, did it?"

"No, it didn't," I replied with a chuckle. "The bosses had already decided that Jerry acted too swiftly and offered me my job back. Actually, another, better position with room for advancement."

"That's great. So you're back at it then?"

"No," I said, then smiled as his mouth popped open. "Someone smart told me that the perfect life probably involves things that make you happy, like a career you love."

He bit his bottom lip and pointed to his chest cutely, and I nodded. "So what then?" he asked, leaning back and draping his arm over the seat.

"It's been a busy week. I'm sorry that I didn't return your calls, but I needed some time to think and get things done."

"Never apologize for that," he said, slipping his fingers into my hair, playing with the strands. "Did it go well?"

"Actually, yes. I organized my portfolio, did a lot of research, set up a website, already booked a family portrait session, and also lined up other job options in case it doesn't take off right away. I'll need to build as I go for equipment."

"I can help with that."

"No, Caleb. I can do this myself. I don't need you to—"

"It's yours anyway. Half of the money from the video. It was yours as soon as you agreed to do this with me. Think of it as a gift from Mer. I'm proud of you, and I know Mer would be too." Before I could respond with more, he added, "So what next?"

"You," I said, abandoning all talk about money and jobs because I wanted him most of all. "You're next. You're always. I love you."

His hand gripped the back of my head as he leaned in. "I love you too, more than anything. You are the perfect in my life."

He breathed the last words onto my lips then took my mouth with his.

I set the daisies in my lap then palmed his smooth jaw with one hand and his shoulder with my other, locking us closer, needing every bit of contact.

Cheers broke through my thoughts of the future, of us beginning our life together. They pulled me back to the present, to the very real crowd still standing below as our bucket went around and around.

I giggled into his mouth, and he groaned into mine. His fingers dug into their grips with a final squeeze before he backed away from me. His eyelids were half closed, his lips wet and sexy. Mmm.

"Don't look at me that way," he said. "This is a family place."

I laughed at the joke, but as his hand dropped between my thighs and his face nuzzled in against my neck, my whole body flashed red hot, and my voice disappeared for a few lustful moments.

"They're—" I coughed. "They're waiting for us to video."

"Right." He kissed below my ear then his tongue made an offering with a long, body-tingling stroke. "I was prepared to stay on this ride all night to avoid them, but there's no chance that's happening now. I need to get you home." He slid back in the seat and wiggled the GoPro out of his pocket after adjusting himself with a smile.

I bit my lip again, excited to go home with him too.

"Let's do this," he said, holding up the camera as the bucket made its way around.

People were clapping, including Nadine and the girls. Caleb twisted the camera, filming the crowd before flipping the lens to face us.

"So we're here at the fair. Some of you watched that leaked video and showed up. I have to tell you that it was unexpected and a bit scary, to be honest. We have no idea why you came." He leaned in and kissed me, knowing all too well why they had shown and giving the camera a little more of it for fun.

"Don't worry, no one's getting Mer's ashes in their cotton candy. We'll leave some of her behind before we take off for the night. But for now, we need to complete this task of kissing at the top of this Ferris wheel, making another check in the list. Mer did it, but Celia and I didn't, so here we are." After we got to the bottom, he motioned and asked the attendant to stop at the top.

When the bucket stopped at the peak, we glanced around, taking it all in.

"Look," he said, pointing down to the crowd and leaning back so I could see. Smashed between several people was a furry blue fox.

"Chances it was at an orgy this time?" I asked, recalling his comment at Merilyn's wake.

Caleb coughed out a laugh. "No telling. You ready for this?"

"Beyond ready," I replied as he popped the latch on the lap bar and pointed the lens at me. "We're doing it Mer's way." We both stood up, holding on to the back of the chair to adjust our positioning on the curved foot area. In the end, we both propped a knee on the seat for balance and to keep everything from tipping out.

Caleb waved the camera, panning around the fair again before turning it back to us. "Come here, my daisy." His free hand cradled my cheek, and I leaned in closer, grasping his chest.

"What, no more Tarsier?"

"Oh, I will never stop calling you that. But you're my daisy too."

The kiss was a crash, brighter than the lights of the fair, the feeling and emotion drowning all the voices and music around us, and better than any other had been. It was filled with passion, love, and promises for a future together, as close to perfect as anything could be. I sighed, gripping him harder to me. His hand slipped down to my neck, and he groaned in almost a frustrated way, unable to hold me fully with the GoPro in his other hand.

"Sit down!" the attendant's voice cut through the cheers from the other buckets and the ground below, and it was all that I could do to stop the giggles from bursting out.

My body began to shake as I held it all in, still staying connected to Caleb's very persuasive mouth, not wanting the kiss to end.

After another second, he broke away with a few quick pecks then spoke to the camera, "And that's another." He helped me sit back down and kissed me once more, chastely but soft and lingering. "We need to see what's next."

"We do," I agreed in a whisper, our faces still so close.

"There are a couple tasks left to finish."

"Yes."

"But no more tonight."

"No, not tonight."

"Tonight, the adventure is us."

Epilogue

Celia

-a week later-

Cringing. I was cringing. Big time. Hearing the buzzing. Inhaling the antiseptic scent lingering in the air.

"You nervous?" Caleb asked.

"Of course," I said through gritted teeth, squeezing his hand.

"Maybe you should have gone first instead of watching mine," he said, looking down at the plastic wrap around his forearm.

"I thought it would be good to watch first. See what was happening, if anything has changed since I saw Mer get hers done. Stop laughing at me," I added when he chuckled. "This isn't funny. You've done this before."

"No, you're right. It's not funny." He cleared his throat and wiped his hand over his mouth to cover his glorious and rather annoying smile. "You don't have to do this. If you're uncomfortable—"

"No, no. I'm doing it. It's fine. It's tiny. Nothing major. Super small. That's all. Quick. Simple."

"Right."

"Right."

"Okay! Are we ready?" Burt, the tattoo artist, strolled back into the room after a phone call, moving to the sink to wash his hands. He was a big guy. It was hard to imagine him working on anything but skulls and crossbones even after watching him do Caleb's.

"Yeah," I said, my dull tone conflicting with the word.

"Cool." He wasn't a guy of many words, which was perfect because he'd gotten Caleb's done quickly and that was what mattered. He slid his hands into his gloves then came over to the seat and placed the transferable sketch of the tattoo onto my skin. "Placement good?"

I stared at the lines, mesmerized by the thought that it would be there permanently from now on, a constant reminder of Mer. "Yeah. It's good."

"All right then. Let's get to it." He checked his gun and lined up the tiny cups of black ink.

There would be no color filling. It was simple. Easy. Would only take like ten minutes as Caleb's had. Tops.

I kept chanting those words in my head on repeat as I tracked his preparation. Buzz. Buzz. Dip.

"Hey," Caleb said beside me, pulling his chair close and leaning in.

I turned my face, and he was right there, his eyes inches from mine. "Yeah?"

"Okay, here we go," Burt said. The buzz of the gun followed and then a pinch against my skin.

I didn't flinch but was about to turn my head to see when Caleb palmed my face and pushed his lips to mine, kissing me boldly and without care. He licked inside, teasing my tongue

237

with soft little flicks from his own. After a minute—or five—of thigh-clenching heaven, those lips traveled over my cheek and in front of my ear.

"I fucking love you so much. You are the sexiest woman on this earth, and I'm the luckiest man alive. Seeing you shine behind your camera again, watching you do all these tasks, and doing this one right now with me … I never thought you could get any more beautiful. You have no idea all the things I'm thinking at this very moment. I want you to move in with me, Celia. Be with me. Live with me. I want us in bed together every single night, not only when our schedules allow. I need you in my arms. At my side. Under and above me when I'm inside you."

"Caleb," I whispered, my eyes closed as he spoke, taking in the feeling of his breath, the sound of his voice. The sting of the tattoo needle was still alive on my wrist, but the rest of my body was red hot, the lovely, erotic scorch of his words seeming to mute all the pain.

"You don't have to answer right now. I thought it would be a great time to talk about it, though." His chuckle tickled my ear.

"Oh, you are—"

"I'm what? An ass. That should be my next tattoo. The word, not the animal or the appendage. Actually, I can think of something better. Maybe I'll get a carpenter bee on top of a little sexy fucking daisy."

I smiled as he pressed his lips to my neck then captured my earlobe between his teeth.

"And that's it!" Burt said.

"That's it?" I glanced down at my arm as he pumped some foamy soap onto my wrist.

"Yep. Not so bad, was it?"

"No," I replied to Burt, mock scowling at Caleb as he grinned devilishly and squeezed my hand. "I barely felt it at all."

"Take a look," Burt said, wiping the suds away with a stiff paper towel.

I held up my wrist and traced the thin lines of the star with my eyes, then the script lettering. Merilyn.

After Burt wrapped my wrist, we settled the bill and got clearance to film at the front of his shop.

Caleb held up the GoPro. "Tattoo task is complete. Let's take a look." We held out our arms, and he swept the camera in close to the clear bandages then pulled back. "These were for Mer. She was a star from the start. All of you already knew. Our supernova. Let's go outside and leave her behind."

We walked out to the parking lot, and he grabbed the urn from inside the Silverado. After choosing a lush area at the side of the building, he filmed me scattering the ashes at the base of a tree then he slung his arm over my shoulder to catch us both in the lens. "What else, Tarsier?"

"This was the last task, so I guess we should say goodbye."

"Right. Last weekend, you got lost with us on that spontaneous Sunday drive we took, so this marks the end."

"We'll be handing this footage over to Jay and Sam soon."

"They'll edit it all up, add in some of the gorgeous pictures Celia's taken too, then put it out there for all of you to see."

"Yes." It all seemed unreal. I stared at the urn in my hands, the lid still off. There was a small amount of ashes left.

"So this is it. We hope in sharing Mer's final adventure with you that you were able to say goodbye to her with us, in the way she wanted. She would be happy. And while you won't be seeing more of Mer on Adventure Life, know that she'd be cheering for you when you have your own adventures. Be safe. Don't do anything stupid," he added with a laugh. "But have fun. Live life. Find what makes you happy. I know we have. Thanks to Mer."

His lips pressed to my cheek, kissing the tears that had streamed down. He shut off the GoPro and let it fall to his side as he looked at me.

"I couldn't dump the rest," I admitted.

"So she goes with us on a few more." His fingers traced the trail my other tears had made, wiping them away. "Special occasions. I have some ideas."

I nodded, loving that plan. "Did you mean it? What you said inside?"

His eyebrows pulled together for a moment. "Every word." He snaked his arms around me and dipped his face down to mine, pressing our foreheads together. "I want you with me every night. I want to be tangled inside this hair while I sleep." His fingers tugged at the ends along my lower back. "And I want to see that gorgeous sleepy look that I love every single morning."

"I want that too," I whispered. "I don't want to waste any more time being without you."

"So, that's a yes?"

"That's a yes."

"It won't be so bad, you and me."

"No, not bad at all."

Bonus Epilogue

Caleb

-the next day-

"**R**AWR!"

"AHHH! Dammit, Caleb."

Acknowledgements

This is always the most difficult part of writing a book. Actually, it's tied with the synopsis. Funny, though, how you can write a book and find it tricky to really express thanks to those who helped you through the process. The words don't ever seem good enough. So, to the people mentioned in this section, you are way beyond awesome, and all the other lame words I might use in an attempt to express how appreciative I am.

Many thanks to my fam, especially Will and Zoe who continuously support my writerly life despite all my random zone-outs, most notably my dinner prep forgetfulness. Take-out it is.

Amy Concepcion—You have a knack for finding those tiny missing pieces and little story blips. Thanks for sticking with me these years. My books wouldn't be the same without you.

Simone Nicole—Girl, you have been one of the best sounding boards for this book and for life. You're truly one of the great author friends I've made in this biz.

Megan Addison—You are a gem and have absolutely made my life easier for this one! Thanks so much for all your help an organization.

Kya Hazzard—Thanks for the read-through and feedback. I'm so grateful for your friendship through the years.

Kim Chance—Thanks for taking the time to read and crit some early chapters during life's hectic schedule.

Emily Lawrence—I can't thank you enough for catching all my grammar gaffes. I probably owe you some heavy liquor at this point.

Stacey Blake—Thanks for always making the paperbacks so pretty. Love working with you.

Regina Wamba—Your skills continue to blow me away, and I'm so thankful to have such a stunning cover photo.

Amy Queau—Thank you for designing the perfect and most beautiful cover to fit SYBL.

Muses (formerly Dreamers)—Thanks for sticking around and helping with all my random group polls and questions. I truly value your input and friendships.

Bloggers—Thanks for taking the time to share your love for SYBL. Your continued support and thoughtful reviews always mean the world to me. Big hugs and much love!

And a huge thanks to everyone who decided to read *Senior Year Bucket List*. I really do hope you enjoyed it!

About the Author

J.M. Miller currently resides in Florida's panhandle.

When she isn't distracted by social media, she writes romance novels that vary in genre from contemporary to fantasy. Aside from spending time with her family, she loves to travel and will jump at the chance to go anywhere, whenever life allows.

Find her

jmmillerbooks.com

facebook.com/j.m.miller.author

instagram.com/authorjmmiller

Sign up for news and giveaways

http://smarturl.it/6s137t

Other books by
J.M. MILLER

Made in the USA
Monee, IL
09 April 2022